C000182651

Black to White

Sam Hayward

Copyright © Sam Hayward 2017

Second Edition

The author asserts the moral right under the Copyright, Designs and Patents Act 1988 to be identified as the author of this work.

All Rights reserved. No part of this publication may be reproduced, stored in a retrieval system or transmitted, in any form or by any means without the prior consent of the author, nor be otherwise circulated in any form of binding or cover other than that which it is published and without a similar condition being imposed on the subsequent purchaser.

ISBN 978-1-9997146-9-7

*In memory of my dearest Leo
for his wisdom, inspiration and most of all, his love.*

Foreword

Losing my husband to cancer was undoubtedly the most devastating experience of my life. The most difficult part was accepting that he no longer existed. How could someone be, then not be? The only way I could make sense of this was to imagine him in a beautiful place where he was at peace, but the question of an afterlife constantly plagued me. I desperately wanted to know if death was the end, or a new beginning.

About a week after his funeral I started to find small, white feathers strategically placed around the house. The first time this happened I was sitting on the sofa in the living room thinking about our wedding day. I went over to the book case and picked up one of my favourite wedding photos then took it back to the sofa to study it. When I put it back, something small and white was lying in the exact spot I'd taken it from. At first I wasn't sure what it was but after picking it up and examining it, I saw it was a small, delicate white feather with fronds radiating from the base, like a shuttlecock. I was so surprised I rang a friend who, to my amazement, had actually heard of this phenomenon. She said they were supposed to come from my guardian angel, but I wanted to believe they were from my husband and that they were proof of his continued existence even though I couldn't see him. From that day onwards, I found them on the kitchen floor, in the bathroom, on my bedside table – even on my leg while driving my car. Each time they appeared, they brought me immense joy and closer to believing that death is not the end. I am also convinced that wherever my husband is now, it is sublimely beautiful and filled with the purest form of love. Whether or not the feathers came from him or my guardian angel, I still don't know, but I do believe that I have had some sort of spiritual guidance since being bereaved.

In 2012 I made the decision to write about my

experience and enrolled on a postgraduate creative writing course at Bath Spa University. Two years later I completed my first novel Black to White. The story is a fictional account of grief which is both sad and uplifting. It also explores the idea of believing in a power greater than ourselves that exists for our ultimate good.

Chapter 1

A gentle breeze lifted the light-blue cotton curtains, allowing a shaft of bright sunlight to illuminate the room. I watched as they billowed out then slowly dropped. It reminded me of the joy I'd once known and the sadness that now clouded my every waking moment.

For some reason, I still slept on the left side of the bed, not wanting to invade the space that was yours. Occasionally my foot or arm would stray over in the hope of touching you but the cold sheets confirmed your absence. Sometimes, if I looked quickly at your pillow, I could see your head still lying there and, if I closed my eyes, still hear you breathing.

The breeze from the open window drifted over my face. It felt soothing, like a hand stroking my cheek and made me long for more sleep but my mind wouldn't rest. Thoughts of the past and what the future might hold whirled around until they made no sense. Then I remembered you saying, 'think of the now Susie. The past has gone, it doesn't exist and the future hasn't happened.' For a while, this thought was calming but then it became clear that you, John Chester, had been my anchor, keeping me safe in life's storms and now I was drifting alone in a vast, empty ocean.

All I had left, at the age of fifty-five, were a few precious belongings to remind me of the life we shared. Your clothes had already gone and everything else I hadn't wanted to keep had been boxed up and given away. It had broken my heart to do this so soon after the funeral, but it gave me some closure. There were no more shirts or jumpers to weep into – only mementoes and memories.

I stared up at the blank, white ceiling and noticed a small spider crawling towards the window. I watched it for some time thinking that even this little creature had a purpose. It had to eat and reproduce – it had to survive. Somehow the spider put everything into perspective for me – I too had to survive.

I forced myself to get up and go downstairs. The heat of the summer sun hit me as I opened the sitting room curtains. It was a day for being outdoors and the thought of working in the garden lifted my spirits. There was something therapeutic about connecting with the life that springs from the soil – watching a seed grow into a plant that blooms, withers and decays was, to me, the cycle of all living things.

I opened the conservatory doors and stood on the patio. It was difficult to remember how over-grown the garden had been when we first bought the cottage. Its transformation had taken eight years of hard work but now as I stared at the drifts of colourful flowers, evergreen shrubs and ornamental trees, I knew it had all been worth it. I just hoped I could maintain everything on my own.

Breakfast was just two slices of buttered toast and a mug of coffee which I took outside to the garden table. The sun hadn't yet reached the patio but I raised the sun umbrella in anticipation and sat down on one of the teak chairs. There were no near neighbours, just a few houses dotted around, and sitting there alone made me feel small and insignificant, like the tiny ant that ran past my foot and down between the paving stones.

I thought back to the previous summer and how I'd helped you walk around the garden. We'd held on to each other as if we were too afraid to let go, but we never spoke about it. Instead we resorted to a perverse kind of humour – making jokes about how feeble you'd become, as if it was something to laugh about. I didn't want to cry so I stood up and breathed deeply, inhaling the fresh morning air. I needed to do something. I cleared away my breakfast things, and went upstairs to put on my old gardening shorts and a t-shirt.

As I climbed the stone steps that led to the shed, my eyes were drawn to my favourite plants – the pale yellow roses that we'd bought during a holiday to Cornwall, the bright pink fuchsias when we'd visited a stately home, and the beautiful Japanese great white cherry tree that you'd given to me on my fiftieth birthday. I remembered we both woke early that day. You kissed me and wished me happy birthday. Then you said you had something to show me in the garden. We took a bottle of champagne and some glasses with us. When we reached the top step and the terrace overlooking the valley, you covered my eyes and turned me round. As soon as you took them away, I saw the tree with a pink ribbon tied around its base and a label saying, 'A beautiful gift for my beautiful wife who doesn't look a day over fifty.' We laughed and I kissed you.

The following year, the tree was smothered in large white flowers that looked like confetti. Now it had grown into a truly wonderful tree with a slender trunk and delicate branches the colour of copper. Its spring flowers had been replaced by small reddish leaves which shimmered in the summer breeze. Beneath the tree lay the pulpy white remains of the blossom.

You had always tried to make my birthdays special. I was so happy that day. I remembered you pulling me close so that my face was pressed against your chest. You often told me how much you loved me. I looked up at the empty blue sky and wondered if you could see me.

The shed door creaked as I opened it. Inside it smelled of earth mixed with old timber. I picked up my tools and put them in a wheelbarrow then pushed it to the back of the fish pond where there was some shade from a cotoneaster tree and started to dig up a huge clump of nettles. It was hard work and after an hour I'd run out of steam. I was also thirsty and soaked in perspiration so I went back to the house where it was cool and a welcome relief, especially the cold slate tiles under my bare feet. I washed my hands then drank a large glass of water before preparing something to eat.

The kitchen had always been the heart of our home with its beamed ceiling, pale, painted walls and hand-crafted units. Everything had been cleverly designed to fit into all the nooks and crannies. Even the Aga sat snugly in the disused inglenook fireplace. Every available space had been decorated with a range of locally-made pottery. There was a quirky, blue and green striped teapot with matching cups and saucers, a milk jug, plates, and a large, plain green cider jug with matching mugs. I remembered you saying that my taste in furnishings reflected my gregarious personality and I wondered if I would ever be like that again.

The thought of doing more gardening after lunch seemed too much like a chore so I went back to where I'd left my tools, put them in the wheelbarrow and took everything back to the shed. It was unbearably hot and all I wanted to do was take a long, cool shower.

As I peeled off my muddy clothes, I stopped to look at myself in the full-length mirror that hung on the bedroom wall. My body still seemed to be in good shape, but my face looked worn and tired and my eyes seemed to emanate sadness. Windows to my wounded soul, I thought and remembered what you had said when we first met. 'You have beautiful eyes Susie, they're like sparkling emeralds.'

It was six o'clock when I left the house and walked down towards the river. We had often taken picnics to a place where brown trout would try to swim upstream. A kingfisher had appeared there once, right in front of us. Its bright blue and orange body darting into the river like a dazzling arrow. It had been a rare and beautiful sight but one that was never repeated.

The early evening sky was ablaze with shades of gold, crimson and mauve, and the sun's weakened rays shone through the overhead trees, making patterns on the road in front of me. All along the verges were drifts of wild grasses, pink Campion and Ox-Eye daisies, and the only sounds that could be heard were the low buzzing of insects and distant birdsong.

Having reached the footpath that led to the river, I

climbed over a stile and jumped down into a field. Just a few miles away there was a main road and the general hum of daily life, but here it was peaceful, unspoilt and hardly known to anyone, apart from local people. In the distance I could see a sparkling ribbon of water.

Our favourite spot was in a clearing where the grass was short and mossy and the twisted roots from the overhanging trees were exposed. In between, there were small burrows made by water rats.

Once there, I sat quietly on the bank, hoping to catch a glimpse of some fish, but the shimmering colours and patterns of the fast-flowing water made it difficult to see beneath the surface. After a while, it seemed futile so I lay back with my hands clasped behind my head and stared up at a large patch of blue sky. A flight of swallows wheeled overhead like small, wind-tossed kites. I watched as they soared up so high they were almost out of sight and then swoop down, skimming the ground as they tried to catch insects on the wing. Somehow I envied them.

My thoughts drifted back to a holiday in France. We were sitting under a vine-covered loggia, reading and sheltering from the hot afternoon sun. You were wearing your straw hat and blue shorts and I could smell the suntan oil on your body. Then I put my arms around you and kissed you on the cheek. You responded by taking my hand and squeezing it as if crumpling a piece of paper. There were swallows dipping into the swimming pool, and all around the deafening noise of cicadas. With closed eyes, I could savour the warm feeling of being with you again. It was so real and comforting I fell asleep and only woke because I sensed the presence of someone else.

As my surroundings slowly came back into focus, I could make out the figure of a man walking towards me. I quickly sat up.

'Hi, sorry to wake you,' he said as he passed by.

'Oh, must have dozed off, probably from too much sun.'

'Yes, beautiful day.'

The man strode on. He was about five feet nine inches tall, fairly stocky and wearing camouflage trousers with a khaki-coloured, short-sleeved shirt. From behind, he looked like a typical hiker with his grey, curly hair, walking stick and old canvas knapsack on his back. It must have been strange to come across a middle-aged woman lying alone in such an isolated place. I watched him until he jumped over the stile and disappeared from sight. His whole demeanour intrigued me. He seemed full of vitality for his age, which I guessed was somewhere between sixty and seventy.

The sun had almost sunk below the horizon and it was starting to get dark when I walked back to the cottage. A feeling of peace had replaced my earlier sadness and I concluded that everything was going to be okay. Life was going to get better. It had to.

Walking towards the cottage, I noticed the man who had spoken to me by the river peering over my gate into the garden. As I approached, he turned to look at me then started to walk on, but I was curious to know what he was looking at.

'We meet again,' I said, opening the gate.

'Oh, hello there, sorry, you must have thought me terribly nosey. I was just admiring your garden. It's so colourful.'

'Thanks. It's been a labour of love, but I do enjoy gardening. There's something very therapeutic about it. Are you a keen gardener?'

'I'm good with plants. I suppose you could say I'm green-fingered.' His soft brown eyes shone when he spoke, exuding a kindness and warmth.

'I'm hoping to find someone who can help me.' The words came out almost without thinking.

'Are you?' He looked surprised.

'Yes, I – I lost my husband recently and I'm struggling to keep on top of everything at the moment.'

'Oh, I'm sorry to hear that. Look, I might be able to help you. My name's Peter.' He held out his large, weathered hand to me.

'I'm Susie Chester, pleased to meet you. Well, Peter, would you like to have a look at the garden?'

'I'd love to. Shall I come back tomorrow? It's getting a bit late.'

'Yes, of course. Sorry. How about eleven o'clock tomorrow morning?'

'That sounds ideal. I'll see you then.' He turned and walked away, looking back just once over his shoulder to smile at me. His right arm then went up in a kind of backward wave.

It seemed strange that he should have come along out of the blue like that. Must be fate, I mused, as I opened the back door and walked into the kitchen. It was almost nine-thirty, much later than I thought and too late to eat a large meal, so I quickly made a salad and took it through to the living room on a tray. TV dinners had become the norm, but far more preferable to eating alone at a large, empty, kitchen table.

My thoughts went back to Peter and how I could afford to pay him. The pension I'd received after your death just about covered my living costs but there was usually enough left each month to spend on a few luxuries. These, I suspected, would have to be sacrificed, but the thought of having help in the garden far outweighed any disadvantages. The day had started in a state of gloom but had ended on a positive note, and I felt I might at last get some sleep.

Sleep did indeed come easily. As soon as my head hit the pillow, I went out like a light, and when I woke the next morning, felt refreshed. This time I got up, opened my bedroom curtains and was glad to see that the surrounding landscape was again bathed in sunshine. Birdsong seemed amplified and a new day lay before me.

Before Peter arrived, I took a quick look around the garden to see where help was most needed. Obviously the banks where the garden was terraced were a particular problem.

7

It was always difficult standing at an angle trying to weed, and after rain, it was usually slippery. Otherwise everything else seemed straight forward. There were six large herbaceous borders with a mixture of shrubs and flowers. The banks were planted with trees, shrubs and flowers and there were two large lawns which needed mowing every week. Running along the entire length of the garden, next to the lane, was a privet hedge which was trimmed once a year, usually in the autumn.

Beyond the main garden, where the steps led up to the shed, was a small area of land that had never been cultivated. It had been cleared of weeds and the grass had been kept down by a neighbour who owned the adjoining field. My ride-on mower would have done the job easily, but he insisted on doing it for me now that I was on my own. He was known in the neighbourhood as Steve the Strimmer, because he would spend at least two days a week strimming his garden and three-acre field. The noise, which sounded like a huge bee, would carry over the entire valley, but no-one complained even though it had become a nuisance. Steve and his wife Beth were too likeable to upset, especially Beth who often called round with a jar of honey or a bag of home-grown vegetables.

I remembered how much you had wanted to create a vegetable garden on this piece of land, but hadn't got round to it. This was something I might ask Peter to do.

I was still outside when I heard the gate open and close, and saw Peter walking towards me. He was wearing jeans and an open-necked, checked shirt with the sleeves rolled up above his elbows. His tanned face was beaming.

'Good morning Susie. Isn't it glorious?'

'Hi Peter, good to see you. Yes, it is. It makes me wonder how long it can last.'

'Well, they've forecast a drought, which isn't good for gardeners, as you know, but I see you're on well water,' he said looking at the top of the well, just beyond the conservatory. 'It shouldn't be a problem, unless the well runs dry.'

'The well takes water from one of the underground springs that feed the river over there in the valley. If the river runs dry then I'll run out of water, but I've been told this is very unlikely to happen. It hasn't been known to run dry for centuries. Anyway, let me show you the garden.'

We began our tour on the lower level and as we walked around, he commented on the plants.

'That's a beautiful clump of Rugosa roses you've got there. They make good hedges, you know.'

I did know, but I just smiled and nodded. He gently touched the cerise pink petals.

'I expect you'd like me to generally keep things tidy for you.'

'Yes, although there's an awful lot to do here, as you can see.'

He didn't answer immediately. 'I can do whatever you want me to. I'm strong and capable. The only problem is I don't have any of my own tools.'

'I have all the tools you're likely to need, including a ride-on lawn mower, so don't worry about that.'

It then occurred to me that Peter was a complete stranger and new to the area and I wondered if I was being too trusting, but he seemed very polite and willing. 'I'm afraid I can only pay you eight pounds an hour. Would that be ok?'

'That sounds fine. How many hours would you like me to work?'

'I think, to begin with, shall we say six hours a week, spread over two days? When do you think you could start?'

'At the moment, whenever you want me to. Just tell me the days you'd like me to work.'

I suggested Tuesdays and Thursdays and he seemed happy with that.

We carried on walking around the garden and I felt he wanted to ask me about my loss. We then reached the cherry tree and I mentioned that it had been a birthday present from you. I told him about your early morning

9

efforts to plant it before I woke up on my birthday.

'He was such a good man,' I said staring at the tree.

'I do understand what you're going through, and I'd really like to help you.'

I looked at him, trying to work out why. Maybe he just felt sorry for me. It was odd, but there seemed to be something familiar about him, as if we'd known each other at some point in the past. I knew this was impossible, but he made me feel at ease, like an old friend.

We walked on in silence towards the fish pond where there was a small rockery, then up a path that led to the uncultivated piece of land behind the shed.

'This is where I'd like a vegetable garden at some stage. John had always wanted to create one here but never got round to it. There was always so much else to do.'

'I'm sure I can help you with that,' he replied, kicking the earth with his shabby leather boot. 'Seems to be a lot of flint here though, so it will need to be rotavated.'

'That would be great,' I said, looking at the impression left by his foot.

There were a lot of questions I wanted to ask him. He obviously knew about gardening, but I wanted to know more about his personal circumstances. I asked him if he'd like a cup of coffee or tea.

'I'd love a cup of tea,' he replied.

We walked back down to the patio and he sat under the shade of the sun umbrella, while I went indoors to make the tea. When I came back, he was wiping the sweat from his forehead with a faded blue handkerchief.

'It really is a scorcher today, isn't it?'

'Yes, better than rain though. We get so few days like this we have to make the most of them. So tell me, do you live locally?' I asked, pouring out his tea and pushing the milk and sugar towards him.

'Not permanently. I suppose you could say I'm passing through. I'm staying with my elderly father at the moment, not far from here. Anyway, I do have some time on my hands and enjoy being outdoors so it's rather fortunate that we've met.'

I found his reply evasive, but assumed he was caring for his father and didn't want to talk about it.

He took a sip of tea. There was a pause and then he asked if I had many friends living nearby. I told him about my neighbours and closest friend Ali. Then, for some reason, I opened up to him, as if all my pent-up feelings from the past few months had found some kind of release. I told him about my family, where I was educated, my career and then about you and how difficult things had been. Tears started to well up in my eyes and I knew if I said anything else, I would cry. I felt confused and wondered how I'd let the conversation focus on me, rather than the other way around.

'It's okay, Susie. Sometimes it's good to talk about these things to a complete stranger. I'm a good listener and it won't go any further, I can assure you of that.'

I felt I'd said enough and tried to think of a polite way to end our conversation. I wanted to be alone again.

'Thank you. I'm sorry I got carried away.' I wiped away the single tear that had slipped down my cheek. My voice began to waver. 'Look, I hope you don't mind, but I've got quite a lot to do this afternoon, so I think I'd better get on. Could I call you on Sunday, just to confirm everything? I may need to do a bit of financial juggling just to make absolutely certain I can pay you. What's your phone number?'

I entered it onto my mobile phone. We then stood up and I walked with him towards the gate.

'I look forward to hearing from you on Sunday. Thanks for the tea,' he said softly.

'Yes, speak to you soon.' I closed the gate and watched him walk towards his car parked across the road. Before he got in, he turned round and smiled at me.

I wandered slowly back up to the cherry tree and touched its trunk. It felt warm and I thought of you. Across the valley a herd of cows was sheltering from the sun under an oak tree, their tails swishing away the flies on their backs. It was so peaceful and seemed like the perfect day for doing very little except lying in the garden and reading. I walked down the steps and into the house to get my book which lay on the coffee table in the sitting room. As I went over to pick it up, I noticed something small and white lying beside it. It was a feather. At first, I just stared at it. There were no windows open, only the door into the conservatory and there was no breeze. I hadn't handled anything with feathers so couldn't work out how it had got there. I picked it up, cupping it in my right hand. It was delicate, like a small shuttlecock and when I held it up to the light, almost translucent. Its appearance was mystifying, but I felt strangely comforted by it. I took it into the kitchen and put it into an egg cup on one of the shelves.

My thoughts turned to Peter and how it would be good to have someone else around. He seemed trustworthy and dependable – the strong, silent type.

At that moment the phone rang. It was Ali.

'Hi Susie, I just thought I'd give you a quick ring to see how you are and wondered if you'd like to go out for lunch on Saturday. It seems ages since we've seen each other. Are you okay?'

'Yes, things aren't so bad.' I told her about finding the feather.

She gasped. 'That's incredible. The same thing happened to my Aunt Joan after Uncle Tim died. They're supposed to come from your guardian angel – how wonderful.'

I'd never heard of such a phenomenon. 'I thought it might have come from John.'

We continued to try and come up with a rational explanation for it but in the end I wanted to change the subject.

'I met a man the other day who's offered to help me in the garden.'

'A man – what's he like? She sounded concerned. 'Look, it's a bit difficult to talk at the moment, perhaps we can chat about this on Saturday.'

'Okay. Why don't you come over about eleven-thirty?'

'Sounds perfect, I'll look forward to it.' She hung up before I could say anything else.

Ali's reaction surprised me but then she knew just how vulnerable I was. I realised I would have to convince her that Peter was trustworthy and, as far as I could tell, not looking for any romantic involvement. He seemed caring and I liked him. I just hoped his stay in the area wouldn't come to a sudden end.

Ali's arrival made me jump. She was always a bit heavy-handed and had obviously lifted the wrought iron door knocker as high as she could before slamming it down three times against the old oak front door. Before she could knock again, I opened it and was pleased to see her smiling face. She came in and we hugged each other. In her right hand was a small, hand-tied bunch of flowers which she held out to me.

'Oh Ali, they're beautiful,' I said, inhaling the scent of the small, pink and white old-English roses.

'I cut them this morning. I thought you'd like them. Anyway, I won't ask how you are because I think I know, but you're looking well. You've got a bit of a tan.'

'Thanks. To be honest, I'm feeling much better. This weather certainly lifts your spirits, doesn't it? How are you?'

Ali lowered her ample body onto the sofa and pushed her long, dark brown hair back over her shoulders. After putting the flowers in a vase, I came and sat next to her.

'I'm fine. Busy with work and life in general, but I've always got time for you – you know that. So how are you coping, sweet pea?'

The warmth of her voice brought a lump to my throat.

'Well, it's odd but since finding the feather, I've been feeling more positive.'

'You'll find more, you know. Aunt Joan kept finding them on and off for two years. They only stopped

13

appearing when she was back to her old self again.'

'How strange but how beautiful – if guardian angels do exist, that is.' I looked out of the window to the fields beyond the road.

Ali patted the back of my hand. 'Perhaps we should go and get something to eat and we can talk about it over lunch.'

'Good idea. Have you booked somewhere?'

'No, I thought we'd try the Three Horseshoes at Hatch End. It's never very busy there.' She stood up and walked towards the door. I picked up my handbag and followed her out into the daylight.

We got into her small, blue Peugeot and drove along the sun-dappled lane. The blur of the passing hedgerows reminded me of the passing of time and how quickly life can change. It only seemed like yesterday that Ali's life had been in turmoil. I remembered the desperate phone calls when her fifteen-year marriage to Simon had fallen apart. It had taken her four years to get over it, but she'd eventually turned her life around by finding a job she loved and moving to a new home. I'd been there for her, supporting her as much as I could. Now the tables had turned and she was doing the same for me.

It was good to get away from the cottage but, at the same time, I felt apprehensive about it. Facing acquaintances was still proving an ordeal. About a month after the funeral a so-called friend had deliberately crossed the road to avoid talking to me. A few weeks later, someone I knew from my yoga class had ignored me in a local supermarket. I'd come face to face with her in one of the aisles but she just stared at me, then turned round and walked off in the opposite direction. Her reaction had been unexpected and deeply upsetting.

Ali put her hand on my arm. She could see I'd gone into one of my introspective moods.

I tried to reassure her that everything was getting better and I was looking forward to having help in the garden. I

14

thought it would be good to have someone else around. She agreed and felt it would give me more freedom, but other than gardening, all I wanted to do was read or go for walks. Socialising was still not high on my agenda.

We pulled into the car park at the Three Horseshoes and were quickly persuaded by the warm weather to eat outside. I wandered over to find a table in the beer garden while Ali went in to get some drinks. The few people already eating glanced over at me as I sat down.

Ali returned holding a couple of menus under her arm and trying not to spill two large spritzers. She put them on the table and gave me one of the menus.

'Here we are sweet pea. Have anything you like, it's on me.'

'That's really kind, thank you – I don't know what I'd do without you.'

She sat down opposite me.

'So, tell me how did you meet this new gardener of yours?'

'Well, I suppose you could say it was fate. I went for a walk to the place that John and I used to go for picnics by the river, just for a change of scene, and must have dozed off. Anyway, I woke up and saw this chap walking towards me. He apologised for waking me up but didn't stop.'

'That must have been unnerving, especially in such a secluded place.'

'Well, yes, but he didn't have that predatory look in his eye,' I said with a grin. 'When I got back to the cottage, he was standing at my gate admiring my garden. We started chatting and he said he was new to the area. He came round yesterday to have a look at what needed doing and seemed a very nice man. His name's Peter.'

'Well, you do have a huge garden and there's no point being a slave to it, so I think it's a great idea. Cheers.'

We raised our glasses to each other and I took a large gulp of the cool white wine and soda, savouring my first taste of alcohol for a few weeks. After a while my head began to swim.

'You're looking a bit flushed,' Ali said smiling at me.

'Yes, I think the wine's gone straight to my head.'

'We'd better order some food, what would you like? I'm going to have the tuna sandwich.'

I chose a chicken panini, and Ali went inside to place the order. When she came back we sat for a while just relaxing and sunning ourselves and talking about the weather, as if we were deliberately trying to avoid talking about anything that might make me emotional.

'Well, what's your news?' I asked.

'Oh, where do I begin? Work's been frantic. I'm organising a conference at the moment which is proving a logistical nightmare. I have to get two hundred delegates from the US, Far East and various parts of Europe to London by October and it's now August. There's such a lot to do, but I'll get there. It's a gathering of environmentalists who believe that climate change is happening faster than they initially thought and that our weather patterns are definitely changing.'

I was about to say something when a young, fair-haired waiter came into the garden holding two plates in the air and calling out our order number. His tight black t-shirt and black jeans clung to his tall, athletic body. Ali put her hand up. He strolled towards us, put our food on the table and asked if we needed anything else. We shook our heads so he moved swiftly round clearing plates from the neighbouring tables.

Ali then started to tell me about a friend of hers who had set up a business making chutneys and relishes and selling them through local food shops and thought it might be something I might like to try. I mentioned my idea of asking Peter to create a vegetable garden for me and that I planned to grow a wide range of produce. But, the idea of standing in my kitchen, day after day, churning out chutneys wasn't exactly appealing.

Ali seemed to pick up on my thoughts. 'Sorry, I'm being my usual insensitive and assertive self. I know you

16

and John had retired and that you never intended going back to work, but now things are different, you might want to eventually.'

'It's okay. I do appreciate your advice, honestly. I suppose right now I just want to take one step at a time and not put too much pressure on myself.'

She reached out to squeeze the hand holding my wine glass. Her touch was warm and motherly. We exchanged knowing glances and then gave each other some space to think for a while.

It was difficult to explain how I truly felt. My life had changed so dramatically I didn't feel part of the real world any more. Everything that had given me a sense of belonging had gone and I was floundering, trying to find something else to latch on to, but Ali was right, I needed to find a new purpose, a reason for living.

I glanced around at the other people sitting in the garden. They were talking and laughing and seemed oblivious to everything else. I wondered if any of them had been touched by loss. An older woman noticed me looking at her and returned my gaze. Her eyes seemed stern and cold, as if to say, 'who are you staring at?' I looked away.

'I'm going to get another drink sweet pea, would you like one?'

'Yes, I think I would, please.' I decided I liked its woozy effect. I also wanted to blot out the negative thoughts that had begun to creep into my mind. Ali took the empty glasses back into the pub.

The sun continued to beat down on the beer garden and I imagined a bird's-eye view of rolling green fields dotted with tiny villages and farm houses. I then thought of you and how fascinated you'd been by the albatross which could fly thousands of miles on one trip to find food for its young. I hoped you were now that bird soaring freely over the southern ocean.

Ali put two more glasses of wine and soda on the table and sat down. The young waiter came back to take our empty plates away.

'I'm sure things will be ok eventually Susie,' she said gently. 'It all takes time, but life has a way of repairing itself.'

'Yes, I know. It's just that I feel so angry about John dying. He was too young.'

I looked at her as if to say I didn't want to talk about this, but then realised it was inevitable. Problems need to be discussed. It's the only way to let go of them and move on. The words 'move on' stuck in my mind. I felt I was on an unstoppable train heading towards the end of life's track, with no way of getting off.

'He was a wonderful man, you were lucky to have married someone who took such good care of you, but you know that. I don't need to remind you. I can understand your anger and your pain, but I'm sharing this with you Susie, so don't ever feel you're alone. I'm here for you.'

'Oh Ali, I don't know how I'd cope without you. Thank you.' I was unable to stop the hot tears from dripping off my chin and onto the table. I searched in my handbag for a tissue but she had one to hand and offered it to me.

'I think I'd like to go home now.'

'Okay, I'll go and settle the bill and take you back. I'm sorry to have made you cry. I really didn't mean to.'

'It's not your fault. I cry at the drop of a hat these days.'

Chapter 2

A cool, salty breeze was blowing in from the south west and a thick mass of grey clouds hung in the distance. The temperature had dropped and it looked as though rain was on the way.

I walked up to unlock the shed so that when Peter arrived he could help himself to some gardening tools. The screech of a buzzard gliding high overhead caught my attention and I watched as it drifted with its wings outstretched in ever-increasing circles then, in a split second, stoop down head first into the field across the road.

At that moment, Peter's car pulled up in the layby next to the cottage. The car door slammed shut and he walked through the gate, looking around the garden then up at me as I came down the steps.

'Hi Susie, how are you today?'

'I'm fine thanks. Good to see you. Those clouds look ominous, don't they?' I said looking west at the dark sky.

He took off his flat cap and smoothed his hair back with his hand.

'Yes, there's definitely moisture in the air which means rain is on the way, but we need it. The earth is rock-hard at the moment. Let's hope it holds off though until this afternoon.'

I quickly thought of the most urgent tasks that needed doing. 'I think it would be good if you could start by mowing and edging the lawns and then we can discuss what else needs doing over a coffee. How does that sound?'

'Perfect. I'll get cracking and see you a bit later.'

I went back into the house, comforted by the sound of Peter trying to start the petrol mower. On the third try, it burst into life and its familiar chug could be heard fading into the distance.

I filled the kettle and put it on the Aga. As I bent down to get the cafetière from a cupboard, something small and white caught my eye. It was another feather. I took the egg cup down from the shelf to see if the original one was still in there, and it was. A tingling sensation spread over my scalp and down the back of my neck. Why was this happening? Where did they come from? I looked around. The windows had been closed all morning.

'Are you here, John?' I said out loud, hoping you would give me a sign, but there was nothing.

A knock at the conservatory door brought me back to reality. I quickly picked up the feather and dropped it into the egg cup and put it back on the shelf. It was Peter.

'I've come for that coffee you promised.'

'Oh, of course, I'll bring it out to the conservatory. Do you take milk and sugar?'

'Just milk, thanks.'

He took off his old boots, leaving them outside then padded across the floor in his socks to sit in one of the cane chairs.

I carried the mugs of coffee through to the conservatory and handed one to him then sat down in the adjacent chair. 'You've done a good job, thanks,' I said admiring the newly-mown lawn.

'No problem. I can see why you need help though. There's a lot of ground here, but it's established, which makes things a little easier. I shall keep things under control for you, don't worry,' he said looking at me with his warm, expressive eyes.

I smiled appreciatively, noticing the approaching storm clouds. It was still warm, but the humidity had increased and it looked as though rain was imminent.

'Could you have a go at tidying up the main flower bed next?'

'Okay, no problem. Shall I put the garden waste on the compost heap?'

'Yes please, if you wouldn't mind.'

He asked how long I'd lived in the cottage. I told him

how we'd scoured the countryside for our ideal retreat to retire to, eventually finding our perfect home, even though we knew it would take years to renovate.

'There's something very satisfying about that though,' he said thoughtfully.

Before I could say anything else, he got up.

'Thanks, I needed that. Must get on,' he said handing me his mug.

Our eyes met and I could see only sympathy in his. I wondered what he could see in mine. I went back to the kitchen but couldn't stop thinking about the feathers. I took the small, green egg cup down from the shelf to look at them again. They were so white they seemed to glow.

Peter was absorbed and quite a distance from the house so I went into the study and turned on the computer. My internet search for white feathers after bereavement produced a surprising number of results. I clicked on one of the links and a list of anecdotes appeared. One of them was from a woman called Sheila. It said:

'I was watching an episode of a well-known soap quite a while ago now which showed the funeral of a little baby. I lost my baby daughter many years ago, but as I watched the funeral, I began to cry as I thought of my own loss. I was alone in the house at the time, and I became aware of something floating down from the ceiling right in front of me. I held out my hand, and the tiniest, pure white feather gently landed right in the middle of it. Since that time, I have had feathers fall at my side, in front of me, and have found them in the most unusual places, usually in the house.'

This was just one woman's experience. Similar stories followed, but there were too many to read. I then imagined you surrounded by a dazzling light. Were they a gift from you? Was there a way of crossing the mortal-immortal divide? It was a mystery which I found both uplifting and unsettling. I shut down the computer and went outside to

21

see how Peter was getting on.

He had swiftly worked his way through the main flower bed leaving it immaculately tidy and had just begun on the next one when the first large drops of rain began to fall. He looked up at the heavens, then at me and shrugged his shoulders.

'I think I'd better call it a day. I'll just get rid of this barrowful of weeds and put the tools away. It seems we're in for a deluge.'

The rain increased its intensity. I helped Peter collect up the tools and carried some up to the shed. He pushed the barrow up the path and dumped its load onto the compost heap then put everything away. We were getting soaked. A few minutes later were shaking off the drips in the shelter of the conservatory. The roar of the rain on the glass roof was interrupted by a huge clap of thunder. Seconds later a flash of lightening cracked across the sky. I offered him another drink and the chance to wait until the storm subsided. He thanked me and went off to the cloakroom to wash his hands.

We sat in the kitchen. Peter stretched out his legs under the table and leaned back in the chair. 'You've got quite a collection of pottery,' he said looking up at the shelves. I told him I'd been a bit of a magpie over the years and couldn't resist accumulating interesting things.

The kettle started to whistle and I got up to make the tea. It felt strange to have a man in such close proximity. It made me aware of an emptiness, deep inside.

'Is your father okay?' I asked hoping he would tell me more about him.

'He's fine, thank you.' I waited to see if he said anything else but an uncomfortable silence followed and I changed the subject back to gardening.

'You've done a great job. I'm pleased.'

'I'm glad. It's a skill you just pick up over time, isn't it?'

'Yes, trial and error mostly, but I think you need a good knowledge of plants to begin with.'

'Yes, of course.'

Again I waited to be enlightened but he was not forthcoming so I drank my tea. He then stood up and peered through the kitchen window.

'It's stopped raining now so I think I'll get going, if you don't mind. Perhaps you could give some thought to your vegetable garden. It would be good to get it done by the autumn so it's ready for next spring.' He put his empty mug on the draining board.

'Yes, I will. See you same time next week then. Thanks so much for all your hard work.' I looked at him trying to work out why he was so keen to rush off.

'That's okay. See you on Thursday.'

He put his cap back on which had dried off from the heat of the Aga and left by the back door. A few minutes later, I heard his truck drive off down the lane.

It was only nine-thirty, but I felt exhausted. The humidity had increased after the storm and the house felt oppressive. I flicked through the TV channels, but there were only game shows and a documentary about fashion so I switched it off and went to bed.

I opened the bedroom window and left the door open. It was difficult to sleep. Thoughts about the future were racing around my head and I couldn't switch off. When I looked ahead, all I could see was a vast, empty void. Yes, I had freedom and I could do exactly what I wanted to – on my own. Life is meant to be shared. No words could express how lonely I felt, but then I thought of Ali and remembered her saying, 'good friends are like stars, you don't always see them but you know they are there.' I'd never realised how precious she was until now.

So what should I do with the rest of my life? The choices before me were endless. Perhaps Ali's suggestion of making chutneys wasn't so bad after all. I was a good cook and the idea of preserving home grown vegetables slowly began to appeal to me. It might even prove lucrative. The thought stayed with me until my mind finally settled down and I fell into a deep sleep.

The next morning I woke to a cacophony of birdsong. One bird in particular seemed very close. I pulled back the curtains and saw a tiny wren on the roof. Its song was surprisingly powerful for such a small bird. I listened to it for a while and thought it had the same compelling tones as a cello – mournful and deeply moving.

Even though the sun had returned, the smell of rain lingered in the air. The grass looked greener and everything seemed refreshed. It was another new day and I felt eager to start designing my vegetable garden. The missing pieces of a puzzle were gradually falling into place. I would make good-quality chutneys with fresh, organic, home-grown produce. They would be branded to look distinctive and appeal to the discerning food lover. I could sell them at country markets and food fairs, even local farm shops. At last, my future looked less vague and I had something to focus on.

As I opened the sitting room curtains, I noticed a yellow envelope lying on the floor by the front door. Just my name was handwritten on the front and it hadn't been sealed. Inside was an invitation to Steve and Beth's twenty-fifth wedding anniversary party, two weeks from this coming Saturday. I stared at the words written in silver. The thought of being surrounded by happy, carefree people left me cold. At some stage in the future I would have to grit my teeth and face everyone again as a single woman, but the thought of being viewed as a sad curiosity, rather than part of a loving couple was unbearable. It was a strange dilemma. In my past life, I wouldn't have hesitated in accepting, but now everything was so different. I visualised walking into Steve and Beth's house and everyone falling silent. I knew they'd do their best to make me feel welcome, but I wondered who else might make an effort to talk to me. It all seemed so daunting. Perhaps they would let me bring a friend. I put the invitation on the coffee table and went into the kitchen.

Glancing through some of my old cookery books

reminded me of the dinner parties we used to have. Some of the pages were still spotted with wine stains. I'd rarely cooked without a drink to hand which had often made me clumsy, but it helped to ease the stress. A wave of sadness drifted over me as I recalled the good times we'd shared with old friends. Perhaps in the winter I would feel like inviting people over for dinner again. Nothing was going to happen unless I made the first move.

There were plenty of chutney recipes to experiment with using ingredients like rhubarb, cucumber, beetroot and aubergine. The cooking process was simple and, as long as the containers were properly sterilised, the food would keep for months. I put the cookery books back on the shelf and sat down to make a rough sketch of the vegetable garden. Designing it wasn't as complicated as I'd imagined and I looked forward to showing Peter when he came back again.

The sound of the phone interrupted my thoughts.

'Hi petal, it's Ali. Just wondered what you were up to?'

'Strangely enough, I've just been designing my vegetable garden.'

'Oh – with a view to making chutneys, I hope.'

'Well, actually, yes. I slept on the idea last night and thought I would give it a try. Now that Peter's helping in the garden, there seemed no reason not to.'

'That's great. It will give you a whole new lease of life. I'm so pleased.'

'Thanks. By the way, I've had an invitation to Steve and Beth's anniversary party in two weeks' time. It's thrown me a bit as I'd like to go, but I'm not sure if I'm up to it. If I can bring a friend, would you come with me?'

'Of course I will. I'm sure it won't be as bad as you imagine, and anyway, you only live round the corner so you can always leave if it gets too much for you.'

'You're a star. I'll ring them this evening then call you to let you know if you can come.'

I felt certain it would be okay. Steve and Beth had met Ali in the past and they knew she was my closest friend. I picked up the phone and dialled their number. Beth answered in her soft, west-country dialect. Our conversation at first focused on me and how I was coping, but eventually turned to the party. She was a gentle, affectionate soul and was more than happy for me to bring Ali, so it was settled – I was going to my first social event since the funeral. The next quandary was what to wear. My dress sense had sunk to an all-time low. I didn't care about wearing anything other than jeans. This was my chance to go out and treat myself to something new and give my self-esteem a much-needed boost.

Ali was pleased she could come with me and stay overnight. We both knew the party would be an emotional test for me. If I coped, then we would know that my life was slowly getting back on track.

I put the kettle on to make some tea. The biscuit tin was almost empty but I reached in and took out two chocolate digestives, eating them in quick succession while thinking about what sort of outfit to buy. I'd lost weight and could wear almost anything, but I wanted to look feminine again. I settled on the idea of buying a dress and knew just the place I might find the right one. Shopping had never been one of my favourite pastimes, but I was now looking forward to it.

The other problem was my hair. It hadn't been cut for months and really needed re-shaping. Well, there was no time like the present. I rang Simon, my hairdresser to make an appointment. I hadn't expected him to be able to fit me in straight away, but he'd had a cancellation and could do it at four o'clock. I looked at my watch. It was only three, so there was plenty of time to get to his salon which was only a few miles away. I didn't hesitate and said I'd see him later. It had been a spontaneous decision but I felt glad. It was the one thing that really would make me feel better.

I had some time to relax so took my tea into the conservatory and sank into one of the wicker armchairs. Peter's efforts in the garden were beginning to show. The lawn looked neater and the flower beds much tidier with hardly a weed in sight. I just hoped he would stay around. It then occurred to me how little I knew about him. He was such a private person, I didn't like to pry, but it was odd that he never spoke about himself.

I thought about my ideas for the vegetable garden and wondered if it would be too much work for him. If it was, then I would have to help, or increase his hours. Time would tell. He seemed to enjoy being in my garden and if his father was difficult to look after, it provided him with an escape. I also felt he liked my company.

I arrived at the salon with ten minutes to spare and sat down on one of the white leather sofas near the door. Simon smiled and gesticulated that he wouldn't be long. He'd recently moved from Surrey and set up a salon in a converted barn, next to the house that he shared with his partner Godfrey. Word of his skills had soon spread, and he was now fully booked most of the time, so I felt lucky to have got an appointment so quickly.

I watched as he charmed his client, brushing her perfectly-cut red hair into its finished shape and showing her the back by holding up a mirror. She nodded, smiled enthusiastically and then got up to leave. Simon followed her to the door and helped her on with her coat.

It was my turn and I was shown to an empty chair on the opposite side of the salon so that one of the juniors could sweep away the mass of red hair lying on the floor. I tried to remember the last time Simon had cut my hair and realised it had been nine months ago. It shocked me to think I had left it so long, but there had been no time to look after myself. I had devoted every spare minute of every day to caring for you. Now it hit home just how hard life had been. What I wore and what I looked like hadn't mattered. At the end you had told me how much you loved me. That was what mattered. The face staring back at me with its shoulder-length, shaggy blonde hair said so much about the past but today that was all going to change.

Chapter 3

I sat in the traffic jam with my foot hovering over the clutch, waiting to shunt forward another few feet. The wipers squeaked as they cleared away the drizzle. Listening to the rhythmic sound of dry rubber scraping over damp glass began to irritate me so I switched them off and turned on the radio. It wasn't long before a local news report confirmed what I had suspected. A serious accident had closed the motorway and traffic was being diverted onto the roads around the junction I had just passed. I drummed my fingers on the steering wheel wondering if there was another route into town, but it looked as though all the roads were blocked so I crawled slowly onwards. As I passed under the motorway, I imagined the carnage above and the families whose lives had been changed forever – just one stupid error causing so much grief. I tried to blot out the sound of the distant sirens.

What felt like an hour later, I turned into the town centre car park and almost immediately found a space. I switched off the engine and sat back in my seat. The journey had been stressful and my first thought was to unwind with a cup of coffee so I made my way to Franco's, a small Italian café I knew just off the main street.

It was busy as usual but I ordered a latte then looked around for somewhere to sit. There were a couple of empty seats by the window so I carefully made my way over, trying not to spill my coffee, and sat down. People were talking animatedly and passers-by were looking at me through the window. I took a newspaper from one of the wall racks, and glanced at the headlines.

The café had a homely atmosphere with its red-and-white checked tablecloths and wooden chairs. Huge framed prints of Italian delicacies hung on the walls and the air was thick with the strong smell of coffee. I peered around to see if I was the only person on my own. There was an elderly man and another woman. It looked as though everyone else had company. Somehow though, it didn't matter. I enjoyed people-watching and could pass long periods of time just observing other people's behaviour. It never ceased to fascinate me.

I'd settled on buying Steve and Beth a silver-plated photo frame. It probably wouldn't be the only one they'd receive, but I felt it was something that would always come in useful. Buying myself something to wear presented more of a problem. I liked to dress up but in a casual way. I needed to feel comfortable, as well as fashionable. A specific boutique sprang to mind and I decided to go there first. Stopping for coffee had been a good idea and I felt ready to face the fray.

I picked up my handbag and put the newspaper back on the rack. As I walked to the door, something outside caught my eye. A small, white feather was floating slowly down past the window. Its gentle descent was so mesmerising and peaceful, nothing else seemed visible and, just for a few seconds, it seemed as though time had stood still. I watched it until it landed on the pavement.

'Excuse me, dear.' The elderly man was trying to get past me to leave. I moved out of his way then followed him to the door. Once outside I searched for the feather. I wanted to find it. I walked along by the window scouring the ground, but couldn't see it anywhere. I then glanced back through the café window. A couple had taken over the table where I'd been sitting and there was a queue at the counter. A man got up and walked towards the back of the café. It was Peter. Even though he had his back to me, I recognised his purposeful walk and wavy, grey hair. He was wearing his usual pair of jeans and a dark blue shirt with the sleeves rolled up. I wondered who he was with.

As I walked along the road towards the dress shop, I couldn't help thinking about him. For some absurd reason, I began to feel jealous at the thought of him being with a woman. I wanted to go back and find out but, if he was, how would I react? I began to wish I hadn't seen him. I also wished I hadn't come shopping. Everything was proving to be such an ordeal.

By the time I arrived at the boutique, I felt more relaxed and pleased to see some stylish dresses displayed in the window. They appeared to be just what I was looking for – plain yet distinctive in soft pastel-coloured fabrics. The shop looked exclusive and inviting with its dark grey façade bearing the name Kara in large, luminous pink, freehand letters.

I walked in and was greeted by a tall, willowy salesgirl dressed in black. She didn't seem particularly pushy and left me to browse. As I slowly worked my way through the rails, I came to one of the dresses I'd noticed in the window. It was a short-sleeved, wrap-over in a very light, silky, duck-egg blue fabric which I thought would show off my tan. I took it over to one of the wall mirrors and held it up against myself. As I looked at my reflection, I had the sensation that someone was standing behind me. It was just a fleeting feeling, but enough to make me see a vague outline of a figure in the mirror. I then thought I heard you say, 'You'd look gorgeous in that, Susie.'

'Would you like to try that on?' The image slowly dissolved into the shop assistant who was smiling at me. 'I think the colour really suits you.'

'Yes, it's a lovely, simple design.' I followed her to the changing room. The dress slipped easily over my body and clung in all the right places. It enhanced my trim waist and the neckline was just low enough to show a small amount of cleavage. I turned to the left and right and let the full A-line skirt swing around my legs and then settle just below my knees. It was perfect. I stood for a while staring into the mirror, hardly recognising my reflection. It had been a long time since I had worn anything so flattering and it made me feel good. If I was to find some kind of happiness again, I would have to make more of an effort and improving my wardrobe would be a good start.

The shop assistant wrapped the dress carefully in tissue

paper then put it in a pink carrier bag. She smiled, looking into my eyes as if she could sense my sorrow and loneliness. As much as I tried to hide my feelings, I knew they gave everything away. The scars of loss ran far too deep.

'You made a good decision. You looked stunning in it. Enjoy.' She held out the carrier bag to me.

'Thanks.' I took the bag and smiled back at her then left the shop. I never dreamt I would have found such a perfect dress so easily – especially one I would be able to wear over and over again.

Finding a picture frame for Steve and Beth proved straightforward too. The choice of silver-plated frames had been limited, so I bought the one I liked best. Mission accomplished, it was time to go home. The traffic noise and hordes of shoppers had begun to make me feel tired, so I made my way back to the car park.

As I walked along the edge of the pavement, to avoid the crowds, I felt a tap on my shoulder.

'Hello Susie.'

I stopped abruptly at the sound of Peter's voice and turned round. 'Hi – what are you doing here?'

'I had a few urgent things I needed to sort out, how about you?'

His eyes met mine and for a moment I couldn't speak. 'I needed to buy something to wear for a party I'm going to next week.'

'That's great. It will do you the world of good to go out and socialise with people again.'

'I hope you're right. Anyway, if I'm not up to it, I can always leave. By the way, I've sketched out some ideas for the vegetable garden. I'll show you when you come again on Thursday.'

'Great, I'll look forward to seeing them. I must go or I might get a parking ticket.'

I watched him stride along the pavement until he disappeared round the next corner. There was something about him that I was beginning to find attractive but I

31

couldn't really define what it was. He was so different to you.

Chapter 4

A sketch of the vegetable garden lay on the kitchen table. I glanced at my watch. Peter would be here at any moment.

The thought of seeing him again made my heart race. I needed to calm down. It was crazy to think of him as anything other than a friend.

I stared at my amateur drawing of eight raised vegetable beds and thought about how life could have been. Images of you and long, summer days drifted through my mind and my heart grew heavy. My emotions had run away with me. It wasn't really Peter I wanted. I was trying to fill the void with someone else, anyone else. I desperately wanted to feel someone's arms around me, comforting me and shouldering my pain. The memory of your emaciated body came back in agonising detail and the horror of watching you take your last breath made me cry out. I tried to stop the tears, but couldn't.

Within seconds, Peter's knuckles were tapping on the small window pane in the back door. I quickly ran my fingers through my hair and dabbed my face with a towel. Before letting him in, I checked my appearance in the downstairs cloakroom mirror. My face looked flushed and my eyes glassy, but I would just have to make up some plausible reason for looking upset.

'Hi Peter. Good to see you,' I said trying to smile. 'Come in. I thought you might like to see my ideas for the vegetable garden, before you started work.'

'I'd love to.' He looked at me with his soft brown eyes and then his expression changed. He'd noticed I'd been crying. 'This looks great,' he said picking up my sketch book. I could see he felt awkward.

Underneath my design, I'd made a list of the produce I intended to grow, together with the months for planting and harvesting. Peter poured over my ideas. He wasn't particularly good-looking and I wondered what I saw in him. His nose was crooked and his mouth was quite small.

I then realised – it was his eyes. They seemed to say so much. There was also something very gentle about him, which seemed to contradict his rugged physical appearance; his movements were slow, almost graceful.

He put the sketchbook back on the table.

'I think I should be able to sort this out for you without too much trouble. You seem to have thought about everything very carefully.'

I sat down at the other end of the table. Peter was staring at me, his head tilted to one side. 'Are you okay Susie?'

'Yes. I just felt a bit low before you arrived. Grief's a strange thing. It's a bit like a tsunami – the waves of sadness can engulf you without any warning.'

There was a silence then Peter stood up, scraping his chair on the stone floor as he pushed it back from the table. I knew he was going to try and console me. My stomach lurched at the thought of him touching me.

He put his large hand on my shoulder. Its warmth flowed down my back and for a moment I wanted to cry again, but I bit my lip and looked up at him.

'Hey, I want you to know I'm here to help in whatever way I can.'

Our eyes met and I could see he meant every word. I also sensed he was not looking for any involvement with me, other than just a friend. As much as I wanted it, there was no spark, no chemistry.

I put my hand up to touch his, but he suddenly took it away.

'Do you have any spiritual beliefs?' he asked.

'Yes, but I'm not religious.'

'So you don't believe in God?'

'No, but I believe in an existence beyond this one.'

'What kind of existence?'

'I'm not sure. I don't know how to explain it. I think there are powers we don't see which are around us all the time. I believe everyone is guided through life. I mean, sometimes we make a wrong decision, like stepping out into the road without looking and we are about to be hit by an oncoming car, and something saves us. The car brakes and you brace yourself for impact then suddenly you fall backwards, back onto the pavement. The car swerves around you and you're safe, and you have no idea how. Why do you ask?'

'To put it simply, you'll never find any atheists on a battlefield. When death stares us in the face, we turn to God.' He walked slowly back to the other end of the table. 'Is it okay if I take this sketch up to where you want the vegetable plot? I need to work out if it's feasible.'

I found his response interesting and wanted to hear more but as usual, he'd held back. I felt disappointed. 'Yes, take it. I'll come up later with a cold drink for you.' He got up and walked slowly towards the back door which I heard him open then gently close.

There was a great deal of truth in what he'd said but I wondered why he'd changed the subject so quickly. It then dawned on me that I wasn't paying him to sit around and discuss religion. Maybe he was conscious of that too.

My thoughts then turned to Steve and Beth's party and who might be there. I hoped people would recognise me. I then realised that Peter hadn't commented on my hair. I walked into the cloakroom and stared at myself, how could he have not noticed? The thick, ragged layers had been thinned and cropped and instead of hanging around my face, they now flicked back, highlighting the contours of my cheekbones. My eyes looked larger and my mouth more pronounced. I looked so different.

It was obvious he wasn't attracted to me. I was used to being complimented, especially when I'd made an effort with my appearance. In a way, it was a relief to know where I stood and be able to forget about any romantic involvement. Life was complicated enough.

I tried not to spill Peter's drink as I climbed the steps up to where he was standing. He took the glass of squash from me and immediately drank it all, then wiped his mouth with the back of his hand and put the empty glass on top of the dry-stone wall. 'Thanks. I needed that. So what do you think of your new vegetable plot?' he asked. 'I've marked out all the beds with some twine.'

I was amazed how big they were. 'Well, it looks like we're going to build a house – they're huge.'

Peter leant against the wall and folded his arms. 'It's going to be a job clearing out all the flint, but with the right machinery, I'm sure I'll manage.'

'Let me know what you need and I'll hire it in for you.' He looked at me for a while and then at the view across the valley. 'It's so beautiful here. I can see why you don't want to move. Are you feeling okay now?'

'Yes, much better, thanks.'

I glanced up at the two large ash trees towering over us, their branches swaying in the wind. 'I've always thought that if there is a heaven, it would be like this.'

His eyes met mine and, just for a moment, I felt an energy coming from them, almost like a pulse of electricity. It wasn't attraction, it was something more powerful which seemed to flow through my body. It only lasted a matter of seconds but felt much longer. Afterwards I felt a deep sense of peace.

'Well, I'd better get going.'

I couldn't speak. He said he would call me to let me know what equipment he would need then left through the garden gate. After he'd gone, I tried to work out what had happened between us. It was so strange, as if our souls had somehow connected.

Chapter 5

The long, tree-lined drive leading to Steve and Beth's was steep and winding. It was also neglected with a few potholes and areas where the gravel had worn away into patches of mud. At the top, where it flattened out, the landscape was transformed by masses of brightly-coloured flowers that nestled against the old flint walls of their pretty thatched cottage.

Above the central porch was the most delicate pink climbing rose that arched up to the first floor windows. Its scent hung in the air around the front door. To the right lay a large expanse of lawn bordered by flower beds filled with shrubs, flowers and a few ornamental trees. To the left was a vegetable garden enclosed by a dry stone wall. The whole effect was enchanting.

Ali put her arm through mine. She could see I was flagging.

'I shouldn't have worn these shoes, they're killing me,' I said, staring down at the narrow ballet pumps I hadn't worn for over a year.

The sound of laughter and light-hearted banter grew louder as we opened the wooden gate. People were milling around a large, white marquee on the lawn and a few familiar faces turned to look at us. Beth was amongst them, and as soon as she saw us, came over to say hello. She looked radiant in a calf-length, white linen dress. I'd never seen her wearing anything other than jeans.

'Susie, my love,' she said softly in her west-country burr and kissing me on both cheeks. 'You look fabulous.' She then turned to kiss Ali. 'Hello my dear. Thanks for coming.'

I gave her a card and my gift wrapped in silver paper, Ali handed her a bottle of champagne and we both said 'happy anniversary,' in unison.

Beth took our presents and hugged them to her chest. For a moment, I thought she was going to cry. She was such a sweet-natured woman.

Steve and Beth had lived in the area all their lives. They had both grown up on farms so were used to a rural lifestyle, unlike John and I who had moved from a city to live the country dream. I remembered how we had struggled with the smell of manure and the total silence of our surroundings. Even the dawn chorus began to get on our nerves. We had been so used to traffic noise and constant activity, it had taken almost a year to adapt to our new way of life, but we knew we could never go back.

As Beth drifted back into the marquee, Steve came over looking red-faced, either from too much sun, or too much beer.

'Hello ladies, welcome to the party. What can I get you to drink?'

We both asked for a glass of white wine and followed him to the drinks table at the far end of the marquee.

My anxieties about coming to the party had given me a few sleepless nights, but as the day approached they seemed to have melted away and I had begun to look forward to it. The sensation of peace I'd felt in Peter's company had left me feeling elated, almost euphoric. I wondered if he'd hypnotised me.

As we pushed our way between the guests, a hand touched my arm and a smooth, deep voice said, 'Hello Susie.'

It was Adam, an old friend of Steve and Beth's I'd met at a dinner party a year ago. I held my breath, dreading the question that would come next. He looked at me for a few seconds before he spoke.

'You look lovely, how's your husband, John isn't it?'

My heart lurched and I looked away trying to think of the right words. I wished I could just say 'he's dead.'

'He had cancer. It all happened very quickly. He died just over six months ago.'

Adam flinched. 'Oh God, I'm so sorry.'

'It's okay. You weren't to know. So, how are things with you? Still tending sick animals?'

He looked at me blankly for a few seconds, then cleared his throat and said, 'Yes, although I'm thinking of retiring.....been thinking of selling the practice.....giving it all up.....I've been doing it too long. I really am sorry. You're very brave, you know.'

He pushed his greying hair back from his forehead. 'It must be difficult.'

'It's fine. I feel fine. Beth and Steve have been so good to me. I wanted to share their happiness. I wasn't going to come, but then I thought, yes, why not? What's the worst that can happen? If I can't handle it, I can go home.'

He put his hand on my arm as if to say sorry again.

When we had last met, he'd told me he was divorced with two grown-up daughters at university. I remembered our conversation about his wife's affair and how she had left him on Christmas Eve. I'd felt sorry for him.

'Can I get you a drink?' Adam asked, noticing that I was empty- handed.

'Steve was getting a glass of white wine for me. I expect he's forgotten.' I looked over to the drinks table and noticed Steve and Ali deep in conversation, their glasses half-empty.

I felt I needed a drink. I sensed that Adam liked me and I was scared. He was very attractive, and I knew I could easily fall for him, but it felt wrong. I was still in the depths of grief, kidding myself that life was okay. Yes, I'd begun to feel happier, but deep down my sorrow was festering like a sore. I knew that just a word or a look could trigger a whole range of emotions. A few days ago I had wanted Peter, but not now. He would always be my friend, but Adam was different.

I looked for Ali but couldn't see her. She must have gone outside. I walked to the edge of the marquee and looked around the garden, but there was no sign of her.

Adam came back and handed me a glass of wine. I took a sip. 'Are you still living in Dorset?'

'Yes, still in the same house, in the same town, but I like being close to the sea. Do you know Canford Bay?'

39

'Of course, it's one of my favourite places. I love wandering along the promenade. I like the sea, but rarely swim in it. It just doesn't look inviting, not like the Med or Aegean.'

'I know what you mean, although Canford's okay. The sea's a bit murky but I haven't suffered from swimming in it, so far. You ought to come down some time. Maybe we could go for a walk and then have a bite to eat somewhere?'

'That would be nice.' The words slipped out before I realised I'd accepted a date with him. A knot of anxiety formed in my stomach mixed with a tinge of excitement.

'I'd like to look around the garden.'

'Do you mind if I join you?'

I shook my head and smiled. We left the marquee and walked towards the vegetable garden. I was keen to see how it was laid out.

Everyone seemed happy, thanks to the heady combination of sun and alcohol, but I still hadn't managed to catch sight of Ali. Maybe she'd gone into the house?

As we wandered between the rows of runner beans, lettuces and tomatoes, Adam looked bemused.

'I thought you might be more interested in their herbaceous borders.'

'Yes, I am, but I've had an idea about growing my own produce so that I can make chutneys, and maybe jams too. I wanted to see how the experts did it.'

At the end of the garden was a bench under an arbour smothered in old English roses.

'Shall we sit here for a while? It would be good to get some shade.'

As we sat down, my leg brushed against his. I moved it away. Adam rested his left arm along the top of the bench behind me. It felt comforting. 'I must confess I'm not much of a gardener, but then I've never had the time. You must have a lot to contend with, if your garden's anything like this?'

'I've got someone to help me.' I could feel the

40

chemistry building between us and tried to distract myself by thinking about Peter. Part of me desperately wanted Adam, but another part of me was denying it. I felt so confused.

'Life's not easy, is it Susie?'

I looked down at my hands. I was still holding an empty wine glass. Suddenly I felt Adam's fingers gently touching my hair. 'It's okay – it's just a leaf,' he said, showing it to me then dropping it onto the ground. I turned towards him. He was smiling. I watched his eyes moving, as he studied every part of my face. For a moment, I thought he was going to kiss me.

'I think we should go back to the party,' I said nervously.

'Okay, if you want to.'

It was the last thing I wanted to do, but I felt so tense and uneasy.

'Give me time, Adam. I'd love to meet you for lunch and go for a walk, as you suggested. Let's not rush into anything. I don't think I could cope emotionally right now.'

'That's fine. I totally understand and I'm happy with that. You just looked so sad.'

We stood up and I started to walk away, but he pulled me back as if he was going to say something else. He then let me go and looked up at the sky.

'It's okay Adam.'

We stood for a while staring at each other with just the sound of distant birdsong, breaking the silence.

'I was going to tell you something, but it can wait.'

'No. Please.'

He put his hands in the pockets of his beige chinos and looked at me.

'I find you very attractive and, when you're ready, I would like to spend some time with you.'

I smiled at him. The feeling was mutual and I hoped he could tell, but I didn't know what to say, apart from 'thank you.' He then took hold of my right hand and lifted it to his lips. The kiss was swift and gentle, but enough to let me know he meant what he'd just said. My heart was racing with excitement and confusion. We were standing very close to each other. I felt guilty. He wasn't you.

'I'd love another drink,' I said softly.

I watched Adam walk towards the gate, then followed him back to the party.

Chapter 6

The room was filled with sunlight. I turned over but the dull ache on the left side of my head and the dryness of my mouth kept me awake. I needed to get some water. The sound of the first bird echoed through the still morning air. It was a blackbird. I rolled onto my back and listened to its song. For a while it continued alone. Then, one by one, other birds joined in.

I pulled the duvet up to my chin and thought about Adam. The party had continued into the evening and Steve had brought out his Spanish guitar. His effortless rendition of Rodrigo's Concerto de Aranjuez had changed the atmosphere entirely and a typically English scene had suddenly become romantic and foreign – even the scent in the warm night air reminded me of Spain.

Adam and I had gone our separate ways after returning to the party, but when the music began, he came back to talk to me. I recalled how we looked at each other. At times, words hadn't been necessary. It was the look that said 'I want you.'

Now, with my head throbbing and my throat like sandpaper, I thought I might have made a mistake. Drink had played its part and I wondered if I'd said anything I might live to regret. The party had ended in a haze but I remembered the walk home with Ali and her constant probing about Adam – her words 'be careful Susie,' still ringing in my head.

I thought of her sleeping in the next room and how she would probably continue the conversation over breakfast. I hoped not. After all, I hadn't arranged to meet him again, although I recalled him putting my phone number on his mobile.

I got out of bed and went into the bathroom, turning on the cold tap and letting it run until the water felt cool enough to drink. There was no glass, so I drank from my cupped hands and splashed water over my face, hoping it might soothe my headache. I took a couple of painkillers and went back to bed. It was only five-thirty so time for a few more hours' sleep, if my body would succumb to it.

Images of Adam, Ali and you drifted through my mind until they became confused. My heart told me it was wrong to fall for Adam, but my head tried to see reason. I thought what you might have done if I had died. We'd always wanted each other to be happy and I couldn't imagine you coping alone for very long.

Almost seven months had passed and, though less frequent, I still felt deep pangs of sadness. Maybe I was just looking for solace in Adam. He'd seemed sympathetic, but maybe that was just to win me over. I needed to get to know him better. We could be friends and more if it felt right. Anyway, he might decide not to call me. This was my last thought before my eyes closed and I fell asleep.

When I woke again, it was daylight. The curtains were open and a mug of tea had been placed on my bedside table. I looked at my watch. It was nine o'clock. My head felt much better. I drank the tepid tea wondering how long it had been sitting there. Ali had always been an early riser.

I got up, put on my dressing gown and carried my empty mug downstairs. My head was still spinning slightly, even though there was no pain. Ali was sitting in the conservatory reading an old newspaper. When she saw me, she gave me one of her 'serves you right' looks.

'Well, I was beginning to wonder if you'd ever wake up.'

I laughed and thanked her for the luke-warm tea then rubbed my eyes and ran my fingers through my tangled hair, trying to make myself look presentable.

'I could do with some toast and a mug of strong coffee – how about you?'

Ali jumped up and manoeuvred me towards one of the cane chairs.

'You sit there and I'll see to breakfast. You look as

44

though you're still half asleep.'

She was right. I still felt very drowsy. I sat down and let my head rest against the back of the chair. I would have probably gone back to sleep if it wasn't for the colourful view of the garden. The sight of vivid pink phlox merging with white echinacea and mounds of purple salvia brought me back to life.

Ali returned with a tray laden with toast, butter, marmalade and two steaming mugs of fresh coffee. We sat at the table and started to talk about the party. At first, the conversation focused on Steve and Beth and how happy they seemed after twenty-five years of marriage, but it wasn't long before she broached the subject of Adam. She'd spoken to him in the marquee.

'You didn't mention me, did you?' I asked anxiously.

'Yes, but only to say that you were my closest friend and I cared about you very much.'

I sipped my coffee with my eyes fixed on her which made her shift uneasily in her chair.

'He seems a good person. Anyone who likes animals must be caring. It's just that I think it's too soon for you to get involved with someone else. What if things don't work out?'

'I'm not going to do anything rash. I might meet him for lunch and a walk along the seafront, that's all.' I could feel anger welling up inside but I knew she had my best interests at heart. She was my closest friend and I couldn't afford to upset her. 'Look, I know how it seems, but honestly, no-one can replace John. I couldn't...'

She tried to smile, but I could see the concern in her eyes. We both knew the conversation was futile. If Adam asked me out, I would go whatever the outcome.

We carried on eating breakfast in silence. I watched her use a piece of toast to mop up the marmalade that had dripped onto her plate.

'Your garden's looking beautiful. Peter seems to be doing a really good job.'

'I know. He's worked wonders. Whatever he touches

45

seems to flourish. He's got the greenest fingers I've ever come across.' An image of his weathered hands flashed across my mind.

Discussing Peter eased the tension between us, but when she wanted to know more about him, it was difficult to enlighten her. He was a mystery to me too, but if he didn't want to talk about his private life, that was up to him. I assured Ali he was kind and helpful, and that I wouldn't be able to manage without him.

After clearing away the breakfast things, I went upstairs to get dressed. Ali resumed reading my two day-old newspaper in the conservatory and began to hum one of the tunes Steve had played at the party.

I turned on the shower and let the warm jets of water soak my face and hair. I wondered if Adam was feeling a bit jaded like me, but then I remembered he had to drive home so probably didn't drink very much. I tried to stop thinking about him. In the cold light of day, I hoped he wouldn't call. Ali was right, perhaps I wasn't ready for another relationship, but, however hard I tried, I couldn't stop the longing inside me. My feelings were being suppressed by a cruel twist of fate. I was in an emotional vacuum where I could only love memories of you. Every day I drifted in and out of reality, trying to remember what being in love was like. Maybe the time had come to start living again. As the soap suds drained away, so did my feelings of guilt and an image of Adam's face slowly re-emerged.

When I went back downstairs, Ali had gone out into the garden. I looked at my mobile to see if I'd missed any calls, but I hadn't. There was no reason for Adam to call so soon.

Ali was sitting by the fish pond trailing her fingers through the water and watching the ripples. As I approached she looked up.

'How are you feeling? You look a lot better than you did half an hour ago.'

I said I felt fine and suggested going for a walk, but she

46

wanted to get home so we wandered slowly back to the house.

'It was good of you to come to the party with me.'

'I had a great time. Thank you for inviting me. Keep me posted, won't you, about Adam.'

'Of course – let's hope he doesn't turn out to be the rogue you seem to think he is.' It was probably the wrong thing to say.

'Susie, you've changed so much. You know I'm only trying to help you.' She picked up her things and let herself out of the front door. Before I could say sorry, she had got into her car and started the engine. As she drove past the house, she gave a quick wave then turned away. I watched her Peugeot climb the hill then disappear from sight.

Of course I'd changed. I would never be the same again. It seemed a stupid thing to say but I knew she was afraid for me.

It was Sunday and although there was plenty of work to do in the garden, I didn't want to spend the day at home. Besides, Peter was due to come again on Thursday so there was no real need for me to do anything. I wanted a change of scene, a walk along the coast somewhere, away from the confines of my house.

It was an easy and pleasant drive to Charcombe, a small cove which nestled between the Dorset cliffs. I first discovered it with a friend and the second time I went there, missed the signpost and ended up on a road that came to a dead end. As I drove down the steep, narrow lane that led to the bay, I opened my window to inhale the sea air. Blackberries were ripening in the hedgerows and clumps of wild flowers still covered the verges. The car park at the bottom was almost empty, despite it being such a beautiful day. I parked and sat for a while taking in the view. Since childhood, I'd always loved the sea. Vivid images of long, happy days spent on sandy Cornish beaches building sandcastles and exploring rock pools came back to me. Time seemed endless then. How things change. Now time was flying by and my life was far from happy.

As I opened the car door, my phone bleeped. It was a text message from Adam. He wanted to know if I was okay and if I was free next Saturday. It was tempting to reply straight away, but I decided to wait until I'd been for a walk. I wanted some time to think.

A cool breeze was drifting in off the sea, but the sun was warm so I left my jacket in the car. I climbed over a stile and started to walk up the steep hill towards a footpath which ran along the cliff top. It was part of the coastal route that stretched from Dorset to Devon and beyond. My breathing grew harder. I wasn't as fit as I thought and the muscles in my calves and thighs began to tighten. Somehow the top seemed to get further away. I wasn't going to make it in one go, so I sat down on a mound of grass to get my breath back.

I lay back and looked up at the sky. A vapour trail from a plane, long since gone, was slowly melting above me. Apart from the sound of waves rolling onto the shore, it was peaceful and I was in no hurry to continue my walk.

Thoughts of the party came into my head and then Adam. I tried to visualise him. His face was well-worn but kind and his grey hair, swept to one side with a very neat parting, made him look like an old school boy. It was his smile and his deep blue eyes that I found particularly attractive. You, on the other hand, were dark and very handsome, and could have passed for Italian or French. There was no comparison. You had swept me off my feet when we first met. It had been love at first sight, until death split us apart. I could never love Adam the way I loved you.

This thought made me apprehensive about seeing him again, but I wanted to give him a chance. All relationships are different and there was no hurry. We had both been hurt and would be on our guard. Neither of us would want to go through such pain again.

The sound of seagulls crying overhead made me sit up. Two fishing boats were heading towards the shore. The breeze had strengthened and white caps had formed on the waves making the boats pitch and roll. It felt much cooler and I needed to get moving again.

It took another ten minutes to reach the path, but once there, the view from east to west was breath-taking. I felt as though I was on top of the world. The beach was a long way below and looking down made my legs feel weak.

A few other walkers were ahead of me, which made me feel secure and less alone. Solitude was fine, but in familiar places.

After almost an hour of steady walking, I felt ready to turn back. My legs were beginning to ache and I'd drunk the bottle of water I'd brought with me. The sun was going down and the last thing I wanted was to be stranded on a cliff path in the dark. I also wanted to send a message to Adam. I didn't want him to think I wasn't interested. The walk had been invigorating and I felt revitalised. It was just what I'd needed.

The trek back took less time and I was glad to see the car park at the bottom of the hill.

When I reached my car, I took off my walking shoes and put on some sandals to let my feet cool down. I checked my phone again. No further messages. I got in and opened the windows, relieved to be sitting down.

My text to Adam said, 'Would love to meet next Saturday. Call me around eight tonight.' I would be home by seven, which gave me time to stop somewhere for a cup of tea. I was thirsty. Well, that was settled. I was going on my first date since losing the man I loved. It was a strange feeling.

As I drove back up the lane, I prayed in the hope that you might hear me. I asked if it would be okay to see someone else. Deep inside, I knew I still loved and missed you so much I didn't know what else to do.

When I opened the front door, my land line was ringing. It

49

was only seven thirty so I imagined it wouldn't be Adam. Before I could pick up the receiver the caller hung up. I checked the number and saw it was Ali so I rang her back. As soon as I heard her voice, I apologised but she laughed and said she was sorry for what she'd said to me, so it had been a misunderstanding. I didn't mention Adam but told her about my walk and she wished she'd come with me.

She then asked if I'd thanked Steve and Beth for the party, which I hadn't, it had completely slipped my mind. It was just after eight so I thought it best to call them straight away before it got too late. No-one answered so rather than leave a message I decided to call again in the morning.

I wondered if Adam had tried to call me, but there was no message so I sent a quick text. He called me straight away.

'I'm so sorry, I've had family here all day and they've only just gone. So, how was your day?'

He sounded harassed but eventually we got round to fixing a time and place to meet the following Saturday. He said he would call again during the week and we said goodnight. Somehow the prospect of seeing him again didn't excite me as much as I thought it would. Our conversation had been stilted. Perhaps it was a good thing or maybe it was a sign that I was anxious.

It was getting late and I had begun to feel the effects of my walk so I locked the doors and went to bed. Sometimes being overtired can have the opposite effect and although my body was at rest, my mind was racing. Eventually I must have dozed off because I began to dream of you.

We were walking along a road holding hands and I was aware of your skin being cold and clammy. I could also feel that your hand was shrinking and slipping out of mine so I tightened my grip but I couldn't keep hold of it. We kept walking side by side but then I was aware of being alone. You had gone. When I woke up, my face was wet and I was lying on your side of the bed. I felt numb.

It was still dark, so I turned on the light to go to the

bathroom. As I walked through the door, my eyes were drawn to something white on the floor under the washbasin. It was another feather. I picked it up and stared at it in disbelief. This time, I was convinced it had come from you. Even though it was so small, it was very bright. If it had been there earlier when I was getting ready for bed, I knew I would have noticed it.

The next time I woke it was daylight. The feather was still on the bedside table, where I'd left it. However hard I tried to explain its appearance, I couldn't so I accepted it as an uplifting and special gift which brought me joy and, for that, I was thankful.

Chapter 7

We'd arranged to meet at the Lighthouse Café on the promenade at twelve-thirty. It wouldn't have been my choice, but it had a good sea view. Perhaps that was why Adam had suggested it. At least I didn't have to worry about dressing up. Besides, we planned to go for a walk afterwards, so I wore jeans and hoped it wouldn't rain. I'd been past the café many times and thought it seedy. Its hoarding had faded and the word Lighthouse had the 't' missing so it read 'Ligh..house.' There was also a lingering smell of deep-fried food which had put me off going in. I thought he might want to impress me on our first date, but obviously I'd misjudged him.

I'd been expecting Peter to turn up at eleven but he'd called to let me know he'd be an hour late. It had been a while since I'd worked alone in the garden.

Although the sun was shining in a cloudless sky, the air was cooler and the leaves were turning from green to gold. Autumn was starting to change the landscape and it surprised me to think how quickly time was passing. It seemed impossible that so many months had gone by. I felt as though I'd been drifting, not really expecting anything from life, yet, I'd met Peter, and now Adam. So much had changed.

A year ago I was lying beside you in the garden, too drained to do anything other than watch some swallows flying high above us, but I was thankful for their amusement at such an unhappy time. Now I was watching them again, only this time without you. A group had perched on the overhead phone cable, chattering like excited children. Others were flying over my head and were almost touching the ground. They made me want to laugh and cry at the same time.

As I was emptying the contents of my wheelbarrow onto the compost heap, I saw Peter coming up the steps.

His broad smile was infectious.

'Hello, I hope you've left me some work to do.'

I let him take the wheelbarrow from me and followed him to the shed to show him the rotavator I'd borrowed from Steve.

'This looks a fine old beast, it should do the job perfectly,' he said, tweaking some of the levers. He pushed it over to the vegetable garden and lifted it onto one of the beds then looked in the petrol tank. A few minutes later he'd got it working and I left him to get on with tilling the lumps of clay that had hardened in the dry weather. His attempts to create perfectly straight furrows made it look as though he was enjoying the challenge.

Beth had asked if I could make some chutney to sell at a charity event she was organising. At first I'd hesitated to say yes because I wasn't sure what to make, but then I agreed. It was a chance to experiment and I thought I'd mention it to Peter. He'd been asking when I was going to get my venture off the ground.

The sound of the rotavator's engine echoed over the valley, but then it fell silent. I took him something to drink. He'd made a good job of breaking down the clay and was wiping the sweat from his forehead with the back of his hand. He looked exhausted and was covered in a fine brown dust. I realised how hard it would have been for me to manage on my own.

'I think it'll be best to leave the beds now and plant them next spring. I'll put some manure on them to fertilise them over the winter.'

His suggestion seemed sensible. It would give me more time to plan things properly and grow exactly what I needed to.

'Beth's asked me to make some chutney for a fund-raising event she's organising.'

Peter was pleased and thought it would be a good opportunity to test the local market. He started to tell me about herbs and how nuns and monks cultivated them for medicinal purposes.

53

'I expect you've heard of the 19th century herbalist Nicholas Culpeper. Well, he believed that asparagus boiled in wine helped to 'stirreth the lust in one's loins,' so to speak.' He coughed nervously.

'You mean it was an aphrodisiac?'

'Yes. Perhaps adding some folklore to your chutneys might help them sell.'

'You're a genius, Peter.'

'There are lots of old sayings, like 'eat sage in May and you'll live for an age' and marjoram's supposed to be good for indigestion, earache and insomnia. Basil is said to settle your stomach and prevent nausea. It's all fascinating stuff. I can lend you some books on the subject if you like?'

I accepted his offer and started to imagine how I could design the labels. A pink heart and the ingredients could be on the front of the jar and a piece of folklore on the back, but I would have to come up with a catchy name. The heart wouldn't be enough on its own. It seemed such a good idea, I was thrilled.

'You seem more cheerful these days,' he said.

I admitted to feeling more positive, especially now I had something to aim for. I also mentioned meeting Adam. He looked away as if I'd said something hurtful. His reaction surprised me. He seemed jealous. There was an awkward silence but then he smiled. 'I wish you well; you deserve some happiness, but don't rush into anything. You're probably not as strong as you think.'

'I'm fine, honestly, and perfectly able to look after myself.' I was about to add that it was none of his business, but stopped myself. He looked embarrassed, realising he might have said something he shouldn't.

'I'll drop the rotavator off at Steve's on my way home, if you like?' Although his comment had surprised me, it was difficult to be angry with him, he was so kind and I knew he was just trying to protect me. He was also hardworking and I didn't want to lose him. I had come to rely on him in so many ways.

He wheeled the muddy old rotavator down the path and out through the gate, and I helped him put it onto the back of his truck.

After he'd gone, I went into the kitchen to look for some chutney recipes. His idea of adding herbs and some folklore about them was fascinating, but the thought of chutney improving a person's sex life made me want to laugh. It would certainly amuse people, if nothing else. As I took a cookery book down from the shelf, the slogan 'a pickle to tickle your fancy' came to mind. I called Ali to tell her, but there was no answer so I left a message.

A few minutes later the phone rang and I expected to hear her voice, but it was Adam.

'Just thought I'd call to see if everything's still okay for Saturday?'

'Yes, of course.' I felt like mentioning my disappointment with the Lighthouse but decided not to. It could wait until we met. Less than a week had passed since we'd seen each other, but I couldn't picture him. All I could remember were his blue eyes and greying hair with its precise parting. Neither of us could think of much to say, apart from we were looking forward to seeing each other. My mind was on other things and he might have sensed that from my voice.

Almost as soon as I'd put the phone down, Ali called and I told her about Peter's idea. She thought it was brilliant. It would involve a lot of research, but we thought it would be intriguing to find out if there was some truth in all those old sayings. She wished me luck and said she would call again in a day or two.

It had been over a year since I'd worked, but the thought of starting a small business seemed far less daunting than returning to a nine-to-five job. I would have the freedom to do things at my own pace. Money wasn't a concern, it was having an occupation and something to focus on that was more important. I'd spent so much time just getting through each day, but now I could see what the future might hold. A new door was opening.

The morning was overcast and cool, but okay for taking a walk along the beach. The thought of lunch at The Lighthouse loomed but I decided to make the most of it. It wasn't the end of the world.

I made it to the seafront car park with half an hour to spare so went to get a coffee before wandering along the promenade. There was a café at the bottom of the main street which had a sea view. It was fairly busy, considering the holiday season was coming to an end but I found a seat near the window. Groups of people were still sitting on the beach fully-clothed and huddled together, hoping the sun would come out.

A couple about my age, maybe younger, were sitting against the sea wall with their heads tilted back and eyes closed. The man's hand was resting on the woman's leg. Every now and again they spoke to each other, their faces almost touching. I watched them kiss then reach for each other's hand. It hurt to watch them. I finished my coffee and got up to go. The thought of seeing Adam cheered me up and made me feel less lonely.

I walked along the edge of the promenade to avoid the bored-looking tourists still wearing t-shirts, shorts and flip-flops, even though it was chilly. I wondered what sort of holiday they were having. All their hopes of a day on the beach had been dashed by the fickle British weather and I couldn't help feeling sorry for them.

The sea looked like pea soup. I hadn't swum in it since I was a child and probably never would again. It just didn't compare with the clear, blue Mediterranean.

My thoughts were suddenly interrupted by the rumbling of a skate board. Before I could jump out of the way, a boy flung himself into me, knocking me to the ground. The edge of the skateboard had glanced my leg and a searing pain shot through my entire body. A crowd of people had gathered around me. The boy was standing holding his skate board almost in tears. He kept saying sorry. At first, I couldn't speak, the pain was too much but, with the help of two onlookers, I eventually managed to sit up. Blood was pouring from a gash just above my ankle and the shock made me cry. Someone pressed a towel against the wound and I heard someone calling for an ambulance.

I said to the man holding the towel, 'I'm meeting someone at the Lighthouse Café. Could you see if he's there? He's called Adam. He's got grey hair, about six feet tall. Please.'

A few minutes later, Adam was crouching next to me.

'Oh Susie, what happened?' He stroked my arm. 'Can you wiggle your toes?'

I could see my leg was swollen but I managed to move my big toe.

'I don't think you've broken anything.'

I tried to smile. The crowd dispersed and the boy with the skateboard had disappeared.

'Well, this isn't the sort of date we had planned, is it?' I said, adding that I was sorry.

Adam put his arm around me. The pain had turned into a deep throb. I leant on him and told him how it had happened.

'You'll be fine, I'm sure. We just need to get you to the hospital,' he said. I could see the concern in his eyes. 'Don't worry about today. We'll do something else when you're back on your feet. Anyway, I'm not going to desert you.'

The ambulance came and Adam followed by car. I was given a painkilling injection before the paramedics saw to my wound. It seemed that apart from needing a few stitches, I had nothing to worry about.

Sitting in the Accident and Emergency Department was depressing. The wait seemed endless and Adam, unable to sit still for too long, periodically went off for walks. He brought me some sandwiches from the café and I thought about what we might have had.

'Not the same as fish and chips at the Lighthouse, is it?' I said, waiting to see his response.

'No, but that wasn't the plan anyway. It was just a

place to meet. I was going to take you to Andre's Bistro off the main street. Did you really think I'd buy you fish and chips on our first date?'

'To be honest, I wasn't sure.'

Adam laughed. 'Well, I obviously didn't make much of an impression on you at the party. No, I wanted to get to know you better.'

'Well, I might be a bit of an invalid for the next few weeks, but it shouldn't stop me limping into a good restaurant.'

Adam smiled and nodded. He suggested a few days rest and then getting together perhaps the following weekend. He squeezed my hand then got up to go for another walk. 'I'm just going to get some more fresh air, back in a few minutes.' He offered to bring me a coffee on his way back. I stared at the nurse on the reception desk, hoping she would have some idea when I might see a doctor. The waiting area was thinning out. She looked over at me and said, 'Not much longer.'

I then remembered my car and how long it had been left in the car park. My first thought was to call Ali. She would know what to do. At first she was more concerned about me but I told her I was with Adam and would explain what had happened when I got home. She said she would sort everything out and not to worry. I told her how much I appreciated her and thanked her over and over again.

When the doctor came to see me, I had almost fallen asleep. He carefully stitched my wound and told me to take things easy until I could see my own doctor. A nurse handed me some crutches and I limped back to the reception area where Adam was waiting for me.

It was early evening before we got back to my house. I hobbled in through the front door and found a note from Ali. She'd phoned the council and told them about my accident. It seemed I would be able to appeal against a fine and she would call me in the morning.

Looking at her note made me realise how good she was

to me and how little I did for her in return. She had a demanding job but she would always find time for me and never expected anything back. It made me want to repay her, take her out for dinner or maybe to the theatre. I would have to do something.

My leg was tingling and I wondered how sore it would feel once the anaesthetic had worn off. I also wondered how I was going to manage around the house.

Adam had gone to get a takeaway and when he came back, I was sitting at the kitchen table. I told him to help himself to a beer from the fridge. He sat down opposite me, poured it slowly into a glass then drank almost all of it straight down.

'What a day,' he said abruptly. He seemed upset that it hadn't gone according to plan.

'I'm sorry Adam. Accidents happen. I'll be okay soon and we can reorganise something. I tried putting some weight on my right foot earlier and it wasn't too painful.'

'Good, but you mustn't push yourself. You'll need to take things easy for a few days at least.' He reached over and put his hand on mine. 'If you need any help with anything, just let me know. I'm very domesticated.'

I couldn't imagine asking him to help me around the house, but I thanked him. It seemed like a genuine offer. He then started to tell me about an accident he'd had some years ago when he'd cycled into the back of a parked car and somersaulted over the top of it. He broke his right arm and twisted his ankle. It sounded as though he'd had a lucky escape. He'd been distracted by a young blonde female wearing a mini skirt and I couldn't help thinking that he'd asked for it. The girl carried on walking and a passing motorist came to his aid.

It was getting late and I tried to stifle a yawn. Adam realised he should go. 'I'll call you tomorrow to see how you are.' He kissed me on the cheek.

'Thanks for everything and I really am so sorry for such a lousy first date.'

'Please Susie, forget it. We'll make up for it another

59

time. The most important thing is that you get better.' He quickly kissed me again, this time on the lips then let himself out.

The only way I could get upstairs was sitting down and hauling myself up one step at a time with my crutches tucked under my arm.

When I reached the top, I looked round for something to hold onto so that I could stand up. The stairs were enclosed between two walls so there were no bannisters. I turned over onto my knees, trying to keep my right foot in the air and somehow crawled towards the bedroom door, dragging the crutches behind me. I grabbed the door handle and pulled myself up. When I reached the bed, I fell back onto it and lay there too exhausted to get undressed.

When morning came, I was still fully clothed. I swung my legs over the edge of the bed and tried to stand up, gently putting some weight on my right foot. The pain didn't get any worse so I gradually put more weight on it until I was standing on both feet. I then tried to walk into the bathroom. I could feel the stitches pulling, but the pain was bearable.

I ran a bath then slowly took off my clothes and threw them into the linen basket. It was an effort but once lying in the foaming, hot water with my leg hanging over the side, I could relax.

Adam had puzzled me. At first he was concerned and sympathetic but then his mood seemed to change when we got to the hospital. He became irritated, as if the whole episode could have been avoided. By the evening, he changed again to being caring and kind. I thought about his brief kiss and that he needn't have kissed me at all. He was hard to fathom but I liked him. I just hoped he still liked me.

I stared at the dull gold of my wedding ring and rubbed off the condensation until it shone again.

Chapter 8

I'd asked Ali to call round after work. I wanted to give her a bottle of champagne to thank her for being so good to me.

Life hadn't been easy for her either. The pain of her divorce had left her bitter and disillusioned but she'd got over it by immersing herself in her job and moving somewhere new. She'd tried internet dating, but the disappointment of meeting men who weren't who they claimed to be proved too much and she gave it up.

In a way it seemed unfair that I'd met Adam so soon and I wondered how she really felt about it. She'd said I wasn't ready for a new relationship, which was partly true, but whenever I mentioned him, she would react as though she resented it.

Her car pulled up outside and I opened the front door to wait for her. 'Hey, you're looking so much better sweet pea.'

'Yes, walking but still slightly wounded – lovely to see you.' My stitches had been removed and the wound was healing well, but it seemed I would be left with a three-inch scar and a permanent reminder of that fateful day which I wished had never happened.

We hugged each other. Ali had swept her long dark hair back into a pony-tail which made her look prim. She followed me into the kitchen.

'So, what's your news?'

'Well, being housebound for the past week, not a great deal, but thanks to Mr Culpeper's book on herbs, I've learnt that asparagus boiled in wine is an aphrodisiac.'

Ali laughed. 'Imagine how many jars of chutney you'd sell with those ingredients.'

'I'm going to try making some to sell at Beth's fundraising event.' I opened the fridge and took out the bottle of champagne. 'By the way, this is for being such a wonderful friend.'

Ali looked surprised, then pleased. She held up the bottle so that she could read the label. 'Let's have some.' She kissed me on the cheek. 'I think we both deserve it.'

'But you've got to drive home.'

'Not if you'll let me stay.'

'I'll get some glasses.'

We both shrieked as the cork just missed the ceiling and the white foam fizzed out of the bottle. I filled our glasses little by little until the froth had turned into a clear, sparkling white wine.

'Cheers.' We chinked glasses before taking a mouthful.

Ali held onto her drink and started to tell me about a scientist she'd met. I sensed from the way she spoke about him that she liked him a lot. He was a meteorologist called David Brookes who had come to give a talk on changing weather patterns at the climate change conference she'd recently organised. I remembered the stress and sleepless nights it had caused, but now, looking at her beaming face it had all been worth it.

They'd exchanged glances in the bar several times before lunch but hadn't managed to speak to each other until after dinner. He was dark-haired, tall and distinguished looking with a permanent frown that Ali thought showed the scale of his intellect. Apart from the impending doom of climate change, they'd talked about politics and other subjects, but the conversation had ultimately turned to marriage and how each of theirs had fallen apart. By the end of the evening, they'd exchanged phone numbers and email addresses.

I topped up our glasses.

'Well, here's to our future happiness.'

Ali hadn't looked so upbeat for a while. She was an expert at concealing her feelings, and it was rare for her to complain about life, but when she was happy, it shone through, and at that moment, she looked radiant.

The champagne made us lightheaded and the subject changed from love to me being accident-prone. Looking back, the whole incident seemed ludicrous and as I retold the story of lying flat on my face on the seafront, we couldn't stop laughing.

Then I mentioned Adam arriving on the scene and Ali's expression changed. I said how kind he'd been and that he wanted to see me again when I was better. She didn't say anything. I shared out what was left of the champagne and thought it best to talk about something else, but Ali wanted to know what I really thought about him. She could sense I wasn't sure.

'Look, I don't want to interfere, but it would be dreadful if you got hurt, just when you're feeling so much better.'

She was about to embark on a new relationship too so we were both in the same situation. When I said this to her, she started to play with her empty glass, pushing it around the table.

'I've been on my own for years now and I could cope if it didn't work out. I'm not sure that you're strong enough yet, Susie.'

I then thought of her in a few months' time saying 'I told you' and that she was right, I would be devastated. What she didn't understand is that my marriage had come to an end unexpectedly. It wasn't a case of falling out of love and fighting until we couldn't stand the sight of each other. The flow of our love had been turned off like a tap. Now I had to contain it until someone else came along. If it was Adam, he would feel the full force of it. He might like it, but then again, might not; but I wanted to be in a relationship again.

Ali was studying me. She understood all too well what loneliness was like, but she also knew how precarious my life would be if I fell for Adam and things didn't work out. I knew it too. I was already anxious about him not returning my phone calls and spending half the night awake trying to work out why. It was like being a teenager again. It seemed crazy that I should have these emotional highs and lows. Everything about my love for John had been certain and I had trusted him implicitly. I knew it would never be the same, but I was prepared to give Adam a chance. 'Whatever happens, I still have my home and security, and no-one is going to take that away from me. It's okay. I know what I'm doing.'

I looked out of the window at the green fields that stretched away to the horizon. It was a view I'd seen hundreds of times but today it looked hazy like the fog of uncertainty building up in my mind.

I didn't hear Ali leave the following morning. Her thank-you note lay on the table, next to an empty mug. At least she'd made herself some tea. The note read, 'Great to see you and good luck with Adam.'

I screwed up the piece of paper and threw it in the waste bin. I wasn't going to dwell on him anymore. It was a waste of energy. I intended to spend the day doing something constructive.

I'd discovered that asparagus went well with oranges so thought I would try making some chutney with those ingredients. After making a shopping list, I got ready to go out. Just as I was getting into my car, my phone started to ring. I searched through my handbag but the answerphone took the call. There was no message but I recognised Adam's number.

On the way to the supermarket, I tried to come up with some names for my chutneys. I was so lost in thought I almost missed the turning into the car park and swerved left without indicating.

The asparagus in the supermarket came from Peru, but it looked fresh and anyway, it would hardly be recognisable after being chopped up and simmered with all the other ingredients. I would use half white wine to half white wine vinegar so that its claim of being an aphrodisiac bore some truth. The prospect of producing something different was exciting. I just needed to think of a good name.

When I got back, I emptied the contents of my shopping bag onto the kitchen table and took out the utensils I needed for cooking. Then, while I was chopping the asparagus, Rosie's Remarkable Relishes ™ came into my head. It was one of those moments when an idea springs from nowhere and feels just right. It had a certain refinement and reflected something special about the ingredients. I also liked the alliteration.

By the afternoon, I'd topped up a dozen jars. I'd tried the relish with ham and some cold chicken I'd cooked the day before and was pleased with the subtle, tangy taste. It had turned out well. The next job was to design some labels so after clearing up, I sat down at my computer to experiment with different typefaces. I'd ditched the pink heart idea in favour of something simple, like black lettering on a white background or vice versa. The message needed to be crisp and clear.

Just as I'd started, the phone rang.

'Hello Susie.' Adam sounded apprehensive as if he felt guilty for not contacting me sooner, but he'd had a hectic week at work and apologised. He wanted to see me and make up for everything that had happened, as if the accident had somehow been his fault so we agreed to meet for dinner. I'd been angry with him for not getting in touch, but the thought of seeing him again made me forget about it.

Working out what to put on the labels proved relatively easy and less time consuming than I thought, even with my mind distracted by Adam and how I would feel when I saw him again. My next task was to sell what I'd made. It was two weeks before Beth's country fair so I planned to try out two other flavours and produce another twenty-four jars. Time would tell if Rosie's Remarkable Relishes ™ was going to succeed or fail.

Adam was due to collect me at seven-thirty. I'd put on some trousers to hide my bruised leg and a long white tunic top to show off the tan I'd managed to keep since the height of the summer. It was six-thirty and as I put on my make-up, I started to feel tense. I was about to have dinner with a man I knew I could fall for, but what if he didn't feel the same about me? It was too late to back out. I sat on the bed and turned on the radio. I felt guilty, which seemed ridiculous. I hadn't felt like this a week ago. The sound of Vaughan William's The Lark Ascending filled the room. It was one of your favourite pieces of music.

There was a knock at the door. I hadn't heard Adam's car arrive. He kissed me on the cheek then stepped back.

'You look lovely.' His eyes moved from my face to my feet and back again.

I'd forgotten how attractive he was and felt myself blush slightly. I thought of Ali and her words of warning and wondered if she was thinking about me.

The restaurant was called The Aubergine. It had only been open for six months but had already established itself as one of the best in the area.

When we arrived we were shown to a table and Adam ordered a bottle of sauvignon blanc. He read out the name and grinned at me; it was the same wine we'd drank at Steve and Beth's party. I was touched that he remembered. The waiter lit the candle on the table before leaving to get the wine. It was busy but the atmosphere was subdued by the sophisticated décor and soft lighting. The floor had been painted a pale grey to match the darker grey walls which were bare apart from some up-lights and several large paintings.

The waiter poured a little wine into Adam's glass but he indicated that it would be okay.

'It's good to see you looking so well.' Adam raised his glass towards me before taking a sip.

'I feel a whole lot better than I did a week ago, that's for sure. So how's your week been?'

He began by telling me how many pregnant cows he'd examined and I wished I hadn't asked. The waiter came back to take our order.

Adam looked relaxed and I could see he was enjoying my company. His expressive eyes glinted in the dim lighting and I couldn't help feeling attracted to him, but I

66

had mixed feelings about what the end of the evening might bring.

I noticed we were the only couple having a conversation. Most of the others were eating in a comfortable silence. I remembered how you and I used to do the same. We were so close we seemed to know what each other was thinking. You would often say what I was about to say or we'd say it at the same time then laugh. I wondered if I would ever be that close to someone else.

Adam was concentrating on cutting his steak. It was rare and surrounded by a pool of blood. I watched him chew the flesh and thought it contradictory to be eating part of an animal he treated on a daily basis. Some of the bloody juice trickled down his chin and he quickly wiped it away with his napkin.

'So, what's your verdict on the food?'

'Excellent. I'd like to come here again.'

He placed his hand over mine and squeezed it. His touch was soft but firm. Our eyes met and the chemistry between us acknowledged.

It was getting late. Adam took care of the bill and we left the restaurant. Our footsteps echoed on the pavement. We didn't say anything until we got to the car and then he said how much he'd enjoyed the evening. It had been wonderful for me too but I didn't say how much I'd missed male company and being taken out for dinner. We got in and drove back towards the countryside. As we approached my cottage, Adam slowed down and pulled into the parking area on the other side of the road. He put his arm round my shoulder and leant over to kiss me. It was just a lingering kiss on the cheek but then he turned his face towards mine and kissed me on the lips. It was warm and passionate and I could feel how much he wanted me. I gently pushed him away and stared through the windscreen.

'I'm sorry Adam. This isn't easy.'

'It's okay. I got the wrong impression. I thought ....'

He stared at me waiting for a response but I looked down

at my lap. 'Oh Susie, look, I appreciate how you feel, I really do.' His voice trailed away. He could see it was futile.

'I do want you Adam. Believe me, I'm as lonely as you are and nothing would make me happier than sleeping with you, but I'm not sure I'm ready to let myself go.'

'What do you mean? Let go of what – the past?'

'Yes, I suppose so.'

He started to stroke my cheek with the back of his hand. 'I can wait. The right time will come.' He looked upset. I felt guilty in so many ways.

He walked me to the front door and as I was about to step into the house, he pulled me towards him and kissed me again. When we stopped, he just held me and stroked my hair. 'I mean it Susie, I'll wait for you. I'll call you soon.' He let go of me and walked back to his car.

I shut the door and locked it behind me then sat on the sofa and wept. The emotions I'd suppressed and somehow denied for so long were now pouring out of me. I groped my way upstairs to the bathroom, wiping the tears away with my hands. I ran some cold water into the basin and bathed my swollen eyes, ignoring the muffled sound of the phone ringing downstairs. I suspected it was Adam. When it stopped, I got undressed and climbed into bed. I lay on my back and as my eyes adjusted to the darkness, stared up at the ceiling. All I could think of was the word 'sorry' until I fell asleep.

Early the following morning, I woke to the sound of the phone ringing again. This time I managed to answer it.

'Hello Susie. I just wanted to check that you're okay.'

'I'm fine. I'm sorry for what happened last night.'

'No, it's me who should apologise. I could see you were upset when I left and realised I might have overstepped the mark.'

'You didn't. I need to take things slowly, that's all.'

'Yes, which is why I said I could wait. I'm very fond of you and really don't want to hurt you. Anyway, I think we've both suffered enough.'

Adam spoke quietly and I could sense his regret. He wanted to come over to see me but I needed some time to think and told him I would call him in a day or two.

It was a dull day, but I opened the conservatory doors and breathed in deeply. The peaceful, distant view of sloping fields, trees and hedgerows reminded me of where I belonged. I hadn't expected to react the way I did towards Adam. It surprised me, especially as I found him such easy company. It seemed natural to want each other, but I still couldn't imagine making love to anyone else but you. It scared me. I had to get to know him. I needed more time, that's all, but I knew that sooner or later we would become lovers and I would have to come to terms with my feelings of guilt.

Chapter 9

There were times when I just wanted to shut myself off from the world. It would have been easy for me to become a recluse and live out my days tending a few goats and growing vegetables. I had plenty of fresh spring water and I had Peter to help me look after the land. He was unlike any other man I'd ever met. He was kind and gentle, but also strong willed, wise and secretive. I found him intriguing. With winter approaching I wondered what his plans would be. There were still lots of jobs he could do. I hoped he wouldn't leave.

The last blooms of summer were hanging on. Their dogged determination made me think of my own fight for survival. I'd come a long way since the day I lost you. The hardest part was accepting that you didn't exist anymore. At first it had been frightening. Everything had seemed so empty. I would listen to my footsteps on the stairs. Even the sound of my breathing was amplified. Noises that I hadn't noticed before, like a door closing or a tap running emphasised my solitude. Being alone was alien to me, especially eating by myself, but that's become bearable now and I've got used to my own company.

I still catch glimpses of you out of the corner of my eye. Certain colours, especially red, seem to appear and disappear. Flashes of you wearing your red jumper or red-and-white striped shirt make me believe I've seen you, but I know this is all in my mind. Old images imprinted on my brain coming alive again. Memories I can't erase.

The garden still brings me joy. Sometimes when I look at Peter, I want him to be you. I want to put my arms around him and just stand and admire what we created. Adam is different, more complex, but I feel drawn to him.

Peter was walking towards me holding a small scythe. I'd been so absorbed I hadn't realised he'd started work. He wanted to show me what he planned to do over the next few weeks so we went to the top of the garden and he pointed out the tree branches that needed to come down and the hedges he planned to cut.

'It seems I'll have plenty to keep me busy over the winter – that's if you want me to stay on?'

I was relieved that he didn't want to leave. 'I wouldn't know what to do without you. You've been such a great help and anyway, I'd miss you.'

He looked embarrassed and laughed as if to hide it but his flushed cheeks gave him away. I put my hand on his arm and felt his muscles tense. 'You remind me, in some ways, of my father and I love having you around.' A warm feeling flowed through my hand and up my arm. There was a strange energy about him.

'I wondered if you'd like to stay for lunch. It'll only be something simple, like a ploughman's?'

'That would be nice.'

'You'll be able to try some of my new relish.'

He smiled. 'Better get on then.'

I went down to the bench that sat in an alcove overlooking the valley. Cumulus clouds were racing across the sky and birds were struggling to fly against the wind. I loved blustery days like this when leaves and twigs would be whipped up and whirled around and the branches of trees would bend until they were almost breaking. It was exhilarating and wild and I felt part of it. Nothing mattered. My worries were being blown away and I wanted to laugh out loud.

I looked up to where Peter was working. For a moment I pictured you. We'd always enjoyed walking at this time of year. It wasn't cold enough for coats, just thick jumpers and boots. We'd walk for hours over the fields and then worry about getting back before dark. When we got home, we'd light a fire and relax with a glass of wine before cooking something to eat, our faces glowing. This thought brought me back down to earth. I went back to the house trying desperately to blank out my memories before they made me cry.

Preparing lunch was a distraction and when I opened

71

the relish, a delicious spicy smell rose into the air. I put a large spoonful next to the cheese on Peter's plate and tried a little on a cracker to see how it tasted now it had thickened. The tang made my mouth water and the combination of flavours worked well. I wondered what Peter would think of it. The labelling on the jar had a quirky Victorian look about it and the word 'aphrodisiac' stood out. I felt sure it would sell, although I couldn't help seeing the funny side. It was difficult to imagine people wanting to have their sex lives enhanced by a relish, but what if it actually worked?

Peter was raking the hedge trimmings into a huge pile ready for burning once they were dry. When I called him, he threw down the rake and took off his gloves.

I opened the conservatory doors so we could look out over the garden and down the windswept valley. Peter helped himself to bread then picked up the jar of relish to read the label.

'Asparagus, orange and white wine....sounds delicious.' He turned the jar round. 'According to the 19th century herbalist Mr Nicholas Culpeper, the ingredients of this relish are believed to be an aphrodisiac. Use sparingly.' He laughed. 'Susie, that's excellent.' He put some on a piece of cheese and ate it slowly, savouring the flavour. He then ate some more.

'This is really good and it's going to sell well, I know it is.'

I laughed. 'Thanks for your vote of confidence.'

'No, really, it is. You're on to a winner. Believe me.'

I thought, from the way Peter was devouring his food, he wanted the relish to work.

'You've got a healthy appetite. Did you have breakfast this morning?'

'No, just a cup of tea. I usually make up for it at lunch time. I think it's good to eat when you're really hungry. You appreciate it more.'

I couldn't argue with that. 'Do you do all the cooking at home?'

'Yes. I do everything.'

His comment surprised me. Peter had never said his father was disabled.

He looked at me. 'You're a good person Susie, and good things are going to happen to you, but please be careful where Adam is concerned.'

I was too stunned to answer. His eyes held mine for a few seconds but I had to look away. I couldn't bear their intensity. I felt angry but knew if I responded, I would say something I'd regret, so I pretended I hadn't heard him and changed the subject. My hands were shaking as I cleared the table.

Peter got up. 'I'll do a bit more clearing up before I put everything away.' He acted as though nothing had happened and as he walked into the garden, he looked back at me. I watched him walk up the steps and, for a moment thought I heard him singing.

The wind had eased and the clouds had merged into dense grey mounds. It looked like rain but not immediately. I heard Peter's car leave. I was annoyed with him and couldn't believe his audacity, but maybe he was just trying to protect me. How gallant. The more I thought about him, the angrier I became. Our relationship from now on would be on a more formal footing and I would keep my personal life to myself. It had been tempting to confront him about Adam, but this time I didn't feel he was acting out of jealousy. He seemed genuinely concerned. It then occurred to me that they may have met. Peter had mentioned his father owning a cat called George.

A few large drops of rain landed at my feet and as I looked westward along the valley, a grey mist had blotted out the horizon.

It was just over a week until Beth's charity fair and I still had more relishes to make. That afternoon, I made another twenty-four jars; twelve more of the asparagus, orange and white wine plus twelve cucumber, red pepper and basil. When I'd finished, my anger towards Peter had subsided. I went to the study to produce some labels. Afterwards I checked my emails and noticed one from Adam. It was two days old.

'Just wondering how you are and whether we can get together again soon?'

I typed a quick reply. 'Yes, I'm free this Saturday. Would you like to go for a walk somewhere?'

The torrential rain spattered against the window. I couldn't stop thinking about Peter's warning and what he meant.

Adam arrived on the dot of eleven. He got out of the car, kissed me on the cheek then opened the passenger door for me. 'Well, the weather's not too bad. Maybe we could go to the country park at Hinton followed by lunch at The Fox. What do you think?'

'That sounds good to me.'

He looked relaxed in his jeans, blue and white striped shirt and grey jumper. I noticed he was wearing aftershave. It was a delicate musky fragrance that reminded me of sandalwood. I said my scar had healed well and joked about our first date being impossible to forget and he told me about the ups and downs of his week at work. It seemed I wasn't the only cause of his moods.

Half an hour later, we pulled into the parking area at the country park and sat for a while enjoying the far-reaching views of a wooded valley. It was peaceful and apart from a few other cars, we were alone. Adam reached over to get a map from the back seat. As he leaned towards me, he said, 'I've missed you.'

He opened the map and spread it across our laps so that we could see the network of footpaths. We chose to walk the five-mile route which would take us downhill for the first mile, along a flat section then up a winding woodland path that led back to the car park. I tightened the laces on my walking boots and got out of the car. The air was crisp and I inhaled deeply. Adam changed his shoes then put on a windproof jacket. He took my hand and held it tightly as if he was afraid I might run away if he let go.

'Come on then. Let's get going.'

His hand was smaller and his fingers were shorter than yours. I remembered how you used to rub the back of my hand with your thumb. It was soothing and affectionate.

The sun broke through the clouds and shone through the trees. We walked in silence for a while, our footsteps thudding on the path, and then Adam said, 'How are you really bearing up, Susie – you know, coping with life on your own?'

I knew he would ask sooner or later. I wanted to say everything was fine but I couldn't. 'I have good days and bad days.'

'I suppose it was a stupid question. It's not even a year since you lost John. I'm sorry.'

'No, life is getting easier and I'm beginning to look forward again. I've come up with an idea that might help me start a small business.' I told him about my relishes.

'Food always sells. It sounds interesting. I'd like to try some.'

His sultry expression made me laugh and I said I'd be selling them on a stall at Beth's charity fair.

'I'm manning a second-hand book stall. Maybe we'll end up next to each other.'

As we reached open fields, the path began to flatten out. Adam went off towards a solitary oak tree and I turned away thinking he needed to urinate, but he called me to come and sit down.

'The view from here's spectacular.'

I walked up the grassy bank and sat next to him.

A panorama of soft, rolling hills interspersed with trees and a few houses spread out before us, like an impressionist's painting. A rabbit hopped onto the path, looked around, then jumped back into the long grass. All that could be heard were the stark cries of a few crows flying over the adjacent field and the wind sweeping through the overhead branches. Adam lay back resting his head on his arm. 'This reminds me of where you live,' he said.

'Yes, I know I'm lucky in that respect. It would be a dreadful wrench to move.'

'You're not thinking of moving are you?'

'No, not yet, but maybe in the long term I'll have to. It's a lot for one person to manage. I've got someone helping me at the moment so things are okay. His name's Peter. You might know him. He's just moved to the area to care for his father who owns a cat called George.

'Sorry Susie, I know quite a few men called Peter and lots of cats called George so without more information, I don't know who you mean.'

It seemed pointless to pursue the conversation. 'I think we should continue our walk.' I stood up and started to walk back to the path.

'Help me up, would you?' He held out his hand to me. As I tried to pull him up, he tugged me towards him and I tumbled over, falling on top of him. He wrapped his arms round me and kissed me. It was warm and passionate. I lifted my head and smiled then rolled off to one side so that we could face each other. We were behaving as if we were twenty again but when I looked into Adam's eyes, I could see those days were long gone.

'You're special, Susie.' He ran the tips of his fingers across my cheek and gently kissed my lips. I closed my eyes and felt myself wanting him. A sudden surge of sadness made me sit up.

'Are you okay?'

'Yes, I just feel a bit emotional. Sorry.' I got up and brushed myself off.

Adam struggled to his feet. 'It's okay. I understand.'

'No, you don't and I don't think it would be fair on you to explain. I'm very fond of you and enjoy being with you, but ....' I let my eyes convey what I was trying to say. He looked away then said, 'I think we'd better carry on.'

He reached for my hand and I let him take it. I felt so confused. Even I didn't understand my feelings so what chance was there of explaining them. All I knew was that I

76

cared for him very much.

'I know how you feel. You're afraid. John's still a big part of your life and being with someone else makes you feel guilty. I can't do anything about that.'

I squeezed his hand and pointed to a squirrel scampering along the path further ahead then put my arm round his waist.

The Fox was a locals' pub and walking in was a bit like entering a private club, but Adam was well-known because of his work. We sat in a corner away from the regulars propping up the bar and the noise of their raucous laughter. 'Well, I'm certainly looking forward to a pie and a pint – how about you?' Adam's face had turned a healthy pink. I agreed and picked up the menu. He got up to get some drinks. As he walked to the bar, he was stopped by a dark-haired man and they started talking. The man looked over at me and Adam turned round as if to confirm who he was with. I smiled but didn't feel comfortable being talked about. The man kept looking at me and I wondered what he found so interesting. It was a while before Adam came back to the table.

'I've just bumped into my ex-brother-in-law, Richard. He obviously wanted to know about the attractive blonde I was with.'

'I hope you didn't tell him too much.'

'Don't worry. I was very discreet. Have you decided on what you want to eat?'

This time I went to the bar to order the food. Richard had his back to me and I managed to squeeze past him without catching his attention, but then I heard my name.

'Susie, isn't it?'

'Yes.' I turned round to see his inquisitive eyes looking me up and down.

'Hello, I'm Richard.' He held out his hand.

I shook it briefly and tried to sound convincing when I said, 'Nice to meet you.' I excused myself by saying that I was on my way to order some food and would catch up

77

with him on the way back but by the time I'd got to the front of the queue, he'd sat down on the other side of the bar and was engrossed in conversation. I walked back to our table without looking in his direction.

'I noticed Richard managed to say hello. I don't blame you for giving him the cold shoulder. He likes blondes.'

'He's unattached then?'

'No, he's married but not happily. Infidelity seems to run in the family.'

I put my hand on his which made him smile. He picked it up and kissed it.

By the time we'd finished eating, the pub had emptied. I'd had a couple of glasses of wine and was feeling pleasantly drowsy so suggested spending the rest of the afternoon at my house and maybe watching a film. Adam was happy with that so we settled the bill and left.

It had been a pleasant day and I'd put the awkward moment under the tree to the back of my mind. There's a right time and place for everything and that hadn't been either. We drove home singing to some old seventies' songs on the radio, both of us struggling to hit the high notes which made us laugh, but at least we remembered most of the lyrics.

It was late afternoon by the time we got back and the light was fading. It had also turned chilly. Adam followed me into the sitting room and I suggested lighting the wood burner. He set to work, crumpling some newspaper then covering it with kindling and a few logs. His fire-making skills impressed me and I thought of an old west-country saying that I'd heard many years ago: 'If a man can't make a good fire, he won't make a good lover.' He struck a match and set it alight.

We sat down on the sofa to relax and enjoy watching the flames roaring up the chimney. It felt cosy and comforting. He put his arm round me.

'I've had a great day. Have you?' He stroked my hair then kissed it. His hand moved to my shoulder and he pulled me close to him. I could feel he wanted me and I knew this time I wouldn't be able to push him away, but being in the house where I had shared so much happiness with you felt wrong. I didn't know what to do, so I just put my head on his shoulder. After a while, he turned to kiss me, this time with intensity and I felt just how much he needed me.

He got off the sofa and knelt in front of me, slowly taking off my jeans. I pulled myself forward and took off my top and bra. He was smiling at me as he undressed and then he started to kiss and caress my body. At first he was gentle but then, as he became more aroused, his kisses became fiercer. Unable to wait any longer, he pushed himself inside me and I felt powerless. Deep down I had longed for this as much as he had and the pleasure was overwhelming. It was only a few minutes before we shared a prolonged moment of ecstasy. Afterwards we held each other and then lay back to rest in each other's arms. I could never have imagined making love to anyone else but it had happened and, at that moment, I felt free. I had to go on living and I knew if you had been me, you would have done the same.

That night he stayed with me and we made love again. When he left in the morning, there were no regrets and I was already looking forward to seeing him again the following weekend, but he said he would call before then.

The next day passed in a haze and by the evening, I felt very low. I was preoccupied with thinking about Adam, but every time he entered my head, so did you, until I thought I might go mad.

Later, as I lay in bed, I could still smell his aftershave on the pillow. I buried my face in it and visualised our lovemaking over and over again. At the time, it had felt right and had given me the release I thought I'd wanted, but now, I wasn't so sure. As much as I tried to justify what I'd done, I felt guilty. The word flashed on and off in my brain until I couldn't think straight. Then Peter's warning came back to me and a cold shiver ran down my neck. Perhaps my grief was more obvious than I realised and he could see I wasn't ready to get involved with anyone else. It would explain the distance he put between us. Ali too had told me to be careful.

Despite my state of mind, I slept but a few hours later, was woken by the sensation of something heavy pressing on my chest. I sat up, gasping for breath and as my eyes adjusted to the dim light of the room, I remembered the dream. A dark figure had chased me through the streets of a deserted city and knocked me to the ground. It was about to attack me but I'd forced myself to wake up. It had no face but I had felt its hands on my body. In the past, you would have comforted me and I would have gone back to sleep but now I was too scared. I turned on the bedside light. I wanted to call Ali but it was too early. Then I remembered the last feather I'd found which I'd put in my jewellery box. I put it in the palm of my hand and examined its tiny white fronds. It was beautiful.

When I woke again, the room was filled with light. It was another new day and I had promised Beth I would help her prepare for the fair. There were phone calls to make and emails to send to remind people of where they had to go and what time to arrive. I also wanted to drop off my relishes so that everything could be taken in Steve's van.

Ali was in a meeting when I called so I emailed her. It was brief, just saying that things had moved on with Adam. He had stayed with me and that it would be good to talk some time. I knew she would want to know more.

Beth was in the garden when I arrived. She put down her gardening tools and came over to the car.

'Hello my dear, good to see you.'

We kissed and walked towards the house. The beautiful rose that had framed the front door a month ago had been severely pruned and the perennials cut back. The garden looked neat but barren and there was a strong smell of wood smoke in the air. Steve was burning all the waste vegetation on a bonfire at the far end of the garden.

We went into the sitting room. The coffee table was covered in paper work which I saw was from the local hospice. It was the charity Beth had chosen to benefit from all the money raised from the fair to show her appreciation for the care of her mother who died there a year ago.

'So Adam Walker is running a book stall,' I said.

'He's got stand number twenty-two by the craft tent. Of course, you know him don't you? I saw you with him at my anniversary party.'

My face began to burn. 'Yes, I met him for a drink at the Fox the other day.'

'Well I never. Susie, I'm so pleased for you.'

'We're just friends, Beth.'

Before I could say anything else, she offered to move me from stand number thirty-four to twenty-three. I couldn't think of a reason why Adam would object to it so I accepted.

Later that day, I emailed confirmation of everyone's stand numbers. Everything had been organised and we celebrated with a glass of wine. Beth looked tired, but relieved.

Adam had sent a text message saying he wanted to see me and Ali had emailed saying she tried to call. Before I had a chance to call her back, I heard the sound of a car. It was a Peugeot. Ali got out and slammed the door. She'd come straight from work. Friend or not, I wasn't in the mood for a lecture.

'This is a surprise. I was just about to call you.'

'You know it's difficult for me to talk at work.' Her face looked pale. She came in and sat down. 'I wanted to make sure you're okay.'

'I know what I'm doing Ali. I'm not eighteen. Adam has told me how much he likes me and I care for him, so we'll have to see what happens.'

'I just felt that you might be upset, but I was wrong. I hope it works out for you.'

Ali knew me far too well.

'How's David? Have you seen him?'

Her eyes softened. 'It's become quite serious.'

'Oh Ali, I'm so pleased. Maybe you could bring him over for dinner one evening. I'd love to meet him.'

'I'll see. He's away at the moment but as soon as he gets back, I'll mention it. I'm coming to the fair on Saturday so I'll see you then. I'm glad you're okay, Susie.' We said our goodbyes and I watched her walk over to her car. I hadn't been able to tell her how anxious I felt, but I was sure she knew.

Chapter 10

A year ago, Adam was just someone I'd met at a dinner party. I could never have imagined becoming his lover. Life is so unpredictable, so precarious. It can change in an instant. He wanted to see me before Saturday so I sent a text saying 'tonight or tomorrow' and his reply was 'tonight.'

He lived in an old fisherman's cottage tucked away at the end of a no-through road, with a small terraced garden that looked out over the bay. It wasn't easy to find but I made it just before dark.

The front door was open so I walked in. I called out but there was no reply. I went back outside and caught sight of him coming along a path on the opposite side of the road carrying a plastic bag. He stopped and took out a large fish then waved it at me, as if to say, 'look what I've caught.' After putting the fish in a bowl of water and washing his hands, he kissed me passionately, holding me close so that I could feel the length of his body against mine. He then led me upstairs and made love to me. Afterwards, he fell asleep in my arms, his gentle breathing corresponding with the sound of each breaking wave.

It was late before we ate, but the meal was simple and delicious. The room was lit by one table lamp and a single candle that had almost burnt down to the wick. We drank two bottles of wine. Adam kept filling my glass, even when I'd said no, so I left what I couldn't drink. He said he wanted me to stay with him forever. At first, I didn't take him seriously, but the look in his eyes told me otherwise and I wasn't able to answer. I still felt uncertain about him.

That night I didn't sleep well. It was a combination of too much alcohol and being in strange surroundings. Adam was snoring softly but I didn't mind. It was comforting to know I wasn't alone. Eventually I managed to drift off and when I woke in the morning, the curtains had been pulled back and the windows opened. A cold and invigorating sea breeze swept over to where I lay.

Breakfast was waiting downstairs. Adam put his arms round me and welcomed me with a kiss. 'How is my lovely lady this morning?'

'I didn't sleep very well, so not as upbeat as I'd like to be.'

He pouted at me as if he was trying to console a child which irritated me. I pushed him gently away then sat down to eat.

'I thought we could go for a walk along the beach, if you'd like to.'

'Have you sorted out the books for your stall tomorrow?'

'Of course, they're in my car ready to go.'

'I'm not so organised. I need to produce some leaflets so I think I'll go home after breakfast, if that's okay?'

He looked disappointed. It wasn't what he'd expected to hear, but then he smiled and said he would reluctantly let me go. 'It's been wonderful having you here. Let's spend tomorrow night together.'

'Okay.' I couldn't think of a reason why not.

It was an early start. Monmouth House was a good half hour's drive away and there was a lot to do. The owners, Sir Ronald and Lady Ann Stafford, had offered Beth the use of their five-acre paddock for the fair and another smaller paddock for parking. Steve and some friends had spent the last few days putting up posters and bunting. It promised to be a good day, especially as the weather was fine. I hadn't got round to pricing my relishes, but the event didn't start until ten o'clock, so there was enough time.

I loved country fairs – they seem so typically English with their beer tents and hot dog stands. There's always a relaxed atmosphere with people wandering from stall to stall or just sitting and watching the world go by.

Beth had organised some Morris dancing and a jazz

band to entertain people throughout the day so I hoped for her sake there would be a good turn-out.

A small gazebo and two trestle tables had been put up for me so I started to unpack the boxes that Steve had left at the back of the stand. Adam hadn't arrived and I wondered if he'd overslept. Sleeping alone last night made me realise I'd missed him.

Beth was rushing around trying to organise everyone, her voice almost at fever pitch. She saw me and started to run in my direction.

'Where's Adam, Susie? We open in half an hour.'

I assured her he'd be here and told her to calm down. Books were easy to display and besides, people liked to rummage through boxes. She waved her hand as if to say 'oh, I can't be bothered' and rushed off again.

Rosie's Remarkable Relishes ™ had taken pride of place on the front table with the jams and marmalade being displayed on the other. I'd brought some dry crackers and cheese for tastings and spread out the leaflets which gave details about Mr Culpeper and the health benefits of herbs. I hoped people would find them as interesting as I did.

Adam arrived with ten minutes to spare before the grand opening. He was pushing a sack truck stacked with boxes over the uneven ground and almost lost the lot when it ran into a dip. I went over to help him. We unloaded the boxes so that he could push the truck out and then reloaded it again.

When we reached the stand, I helped him set out the books. Every so often he patted my behind or put his arm round me. He then dashed over to my stall to eat a cracker or a lump of cheese. If I told him off he became more annoying and I began to wish I wasn't on the next stand.

People started coming through the gates. Sir Ronald and his wife were talking to Beth and Steve. As more and more visitors arrived, Sir Ronald mounted a podium and tested his microphone. Everyone stopped and looked in his direction. His voice echoed as he spoke about the work of the local hospice which he said was a very deserving cause. He then declared the fair open and wished everyone a successful and enjoyable day.

Adam was soon surrounded by book lovers searching for a bargain but my relishes started to attract a small crowd. Everyone who sampled the asparagus, orange and white wine bought a jar and took a leaflet to find out more about its aphrodisiac properties. There were shrieks and peals of laughter as sex became the main talking point. Peter's idea had worked. By lunchtime I'd sold out, apart from two jars, which I kept back for tastings. People were still taking leaflets which enabled them to order by post, email or phone and I wondered how I might cope if I was inundated. Adam kept looking over at me and when he managed to catch my attention, he mouthed, 'well done.'

As people wandered away, I had a chance to look around. The bric-a-brac stalls were still busy and a large crowd had gathered outside the beer tent. A man wearing a straw hat was standing by the entrance. He was staring in my direction. He took off his hat and I realised it was Peter. I asked Adam to mind my stall for a few minutes. I pushed my way through the crowds but when I got near to where he'd been standing, he'd gone. I looked inside the beer tent but there was no sign of him. I'd wanted so much to tell him about my success. I went back into the tent and bought two pints of lager then carried them back to the stall.

Adam took the drinks and put them on the table. He put his arms round me and kissed me on the forehead.

'Who's a clever girl then?'

'I suppose I am.'

'What's up? I thought you'd be over the moon.'

'I'm thrilled but also a bit overwhelmed.' I gently pushed him away. Peter's disappearance was odd, as if he deliberately tried to avoid me. I wondered if Adam was the reason.

Adam almost downed his lager in one then went off to buy something to eat. The smell of fried onions and chargrilled meat had made us both hungry.

I picked up one of the books on Adam's stall. It was Hardy's love story 'A Pair of Blue Eyes' which I'd read many years ago and now, re-reading the first page, realised why I hadn't enjoyed it.

'I see you've had a good day.' I quickly put the book down and was pleased to see Ali. She was standing next to a tall, good-looking man who I assumed to be David. I held out my hand and introduced myself and he reciprocated saying that he'd heard a lot about me.

'....All positive I hope,' I said looking at Ali.

He smiled and I understood why she was so attracted to him. His sparkling eyes exuded warmth and intelligence. He picked up one of my leaflets and quoted the piece about my relish being an aphrodisiac. He then put his arm around Ali.

'No wonder you've sold out.'

I said I'd be making more and giving some to Ali for her much-valued opinion.

'I'll let you know if it does what it says on the jar.' She laughed. David looked coyly at his feet.

Adam came back holding a beef burger in a napkin. The corners of his mouth showed traces of tomato ketchup and I guessed he'd already eaten his. He said hello to Ali then introduced himself to David, shaking his hand. They seemed to get on immediately and walked over to his stall to talk about books.

'Ali, he's lovely.'

'Yes. Fingers crossed. How are things between you and Adam?'

'Okay, although he can be a little annoying at times. He means well and is very affectionate.' I started to eat my beef burger.

'We should arrange that dinner party.'

The two men were deep in conversation about the environment and politics. Ali and I left them to it and went for a walk. I looked back at Adam and nodded in the direction of my stall.

'I'll talk to Adam tonight about it. I'm sure we'll be able to organise something.'

Ali smiled and began to tell me about David. They were spending more and more time together and from the way she spoke about him, I sensed she'd fallen in love. I wondered if he felt the same. I then thought about our friendship and what might happen if they moved in together. I hoped she wouldn't abandon me. In a way I felt resentful but then realised how selfish I was being. How could I possibly object? She had been through so much. I tried to hide my feelings by saying I wished her all the happiness in the world.

We wandered aimlessly then stopped to look at some handmade jewellery and vintage clothing. Ali pulled out a straight, black crepe dress with a lace bodice. It looked very 1970s. She held it up against herself and I could see it would be too tight, but she insisted on trying it on in the makeshift cubicle. Her cry of 'oh God' confirmed what I'd suspected. She opened the curtains and I shook my head. There were far too many bulges. Our eyes met and we burst out laughing.

We strolled towards the beer tent and I found somewhere to sit while Ali went in to buy some drinks. It was late afternoon and people were beginning to leave. The fair had been a success and I felt pleased for Beth. Everyone had agreed to sell their goods on a fifty-fifty basis and I wondered how much money had been raised – if my takings were anything to go by, quite a lot.

Ali came back with two glasses of wine. The conversation went back to Adam and what I thought might come of our relationship. She had a way of probing that made me open up to her but on this occasion I became defensive. I didn't know him well enough to make a judgement. He was good company and I missed him when I wasn't with him, but it was far too soon to think about anything more permanent. I changed the subject to Peter and pointed to the spot where he'd been standing. I explained how he'd been staring at me but when I went over to talk to him, he'd gone and I hadn't been able to find him. She thought it was strange and when I mentioned his warning about Adam, she looked anxious.

'I think he's jealous. I hope he's not stalking you Susie.'

Her comment disturbed me. He was unusually secretive but I tried to convince her that he'd never shown an interest in me. I told her how he'd flinched when I'd touched his arm and that he didn't like physical contact, but she stared at me, as if to say, maybe he did. It was hard to believe Peter would do anything to hurt me. He'd helped me so much.

The last few visitors were making their way to the exit. As we walked back to the stall, we could see Adam and David still deep in conversation. They were obviously getting on well and the thought of having dinner together seemed increasingly like a good idea.

'Where have you been? We thought you'd abandoned us.' Adam was standing with his hands on his hips trying to look annoyed, but he couldn't help smiling. He pulled me towards him and hugged me. 'I missed you.'

Ali put her arm through David's and he kissed her cheek. He then turned to Adam and shook his hand saying how much he'd enjoyed their discussion and hoped they would meet again.

'Why don't you come over for dinner?' I said, thinking it was an opportune moment to arrange something.

'That would be great.' David looked at Ali.

'Okay. Susie and I will fix a date.'

I kissed Ali goodbye and told David I looked forward to meeting him again. As they walked away, I noticed a couple of books under David's arm and smiled at Adam. 'You're a great salesman. I'm impressed.'

'…Never known to miss an opportunity.'

It didn't take long to pack up. I put our takings in my shoulder bag then helped to load the few remaining boxes onto the sack truck which Adam trundled towards the gate. Beth was talking to some stallholders and as we passed, she waved and gesticulated that she would phone me.

By the time we got back to the cottage, it was dark. The sitting room was still warm, even though the fire had gone out. Adam put some newspaper and kindling on the embers and lit them. After putting on a few logs, he came and sat next to me on the sofa. I lay my head on his shoulder and he put his arm round me. We sat quietly absorbed in our own thoughts. It reminded me of those contented moments you and I had shared and I wondered if I would fall in love with him. I knew I had to let go of the past but I didn't want to give in to him completely, not yet. Peter's warning still worried me. I wondered what he knew about Adam that I didn't. Perhaps I would find out in time but tonight I just wanted to enjoy his company and the warmth of his bed.

The brass carriage clock on the mantelpiece chimed seven. Adam was still dozing with his arm round me so I moved it gently away and got up. I put some more logs on the fire and a sudden crack made him wake up. He yawned and muttered about being hungry. It was too late to cook so I suggested driving down to the harbour to get some fish and chips. The wind had got up. Each gust made the windows rattle and the sound of waves crashing onto the shore had become a constant roar.

Just as I was about to open the car door, Adam said, 'Let's walk along by the sea. It'll be exciting.'

'It's too dark,' I replied anxiously.

He went back to the house to get a torch and then started to walk down the path to the beach.

At first I hesitated then followed him. It was a more direct route to the harbour and would be quicker than going by car, but the wildness of the sea frightened me. When we got to the beach, the noise was deafening and we could hardly hear each other speak. Adam pulled me towards him and held me close, protecting me from the spray thrown up by each breaking wave. Our feet sank into the shingle.

'I love the sea when it's like this. It's exhilarating.' He

shone the torch towards it so we could see the enormous breakers only about twenty feet away. I just hoped there wouldn't be a rogue wave that surged in and swamped us.

The lights of the harbour eventually came into view and the bay curved away. It was a relief to know we were heading towards safety. I'd always had great respect for the sea and knew how dangerous it could be. Walking under cliffs in the dark and not knowing the state of the tide had been foolish and I was angry with Adam for persuading me to do it.

'Can we get a taxi back?'

Adam rolled his eyes.

'I'm not walking back along the beach, it's too dangerous.'

'Don't be ridiculous.'

'You don't know whether the tide's coming in or going out. We could get trapped.'

He laughed and I tried to run away from him, but he caught up with me and took hold of my arm. 'Susie, what on earth's the matter with you?'

'You can find your own way back, I'm taking a taxi.' I wrenched my arm away.

'Oh sweetheart, don't be angry with me. I'm so sorry. Forgive me. I would never do anything to hurt you. I love you.' He looked at me, searching my face as if he was afraid of what he'd just said. I couldn't answer. The silence was agonising so I kissed him briefly on the lips.

'Can we get a taxi home then?'

'Yes.' His eyes had lost their excitement.

We continued walking hand in hand until we reached the promenade and a fish and chip kiosk. About a hundred yards further on, I saw the half-lit sign for The Lighthouse Café and wondered what might have happened that day if I hadn't had my accident. The wind moaned as it tore through the rigging of some yachts moored nearby and the free-standing 'fish and chips' sign suddenly blew over. I picked it up and put it against the side of the kiosk. Adam ordered our food and I looked around for a taxi. There was only one waiting in the rank so I ran over, spoke to the driver and got in. He picked Adam up on the way past and began to complain about the smell of fish and chips lingering in his cab so we opened the windows but he complained about that too. We reached the cottage before he could complain about anything else and, as we got out, Adam offered him a chip. He scowled, shook his head then drove off at high speed.

By the time we'd eaten, it was almost nine o'clock. Adam poured himself a beer and a glass of wine for me. He seemed moody, as if he was still sulking over what happened on the beach. He'd told me he loved me and I hadn't reciprocated. The atmosphere was tense. After we'd finished, he said, 'I think we need to clear the air, Susie.'

'What do you mean?'

'Perhaps this isn't going to work.'

The words cut into me. 'Why?'

'..Because I'm not sure how you feel about me.'

I tried to explain that I needed more time, but he didn't want to hear that excuse anymore. Anger welled up inside me. I went into the sitting room and sat in an armchair by the fire. Adam stayed in the kitchen. I heard him open another beer. He then came through and sat in the opposite armchair. I felt hurt that he'd not offered me another drink so I made a point of saying that I was going to get a glass of wine. When I came back, he was standing in front of the fire with his back to me and I sensed he wanted me to go. Before he could say anything, I asked him if that was what he wanted, and he suddenly spun round. 'No, I don't.' He took my drink from me and put it on the mantelpiece then pulled me into his arms and kissed me with such intensity, I could barely breathe. He pushed me over to the sofa and I fell back, but before I could sit up, he was on top of me, grappling with the zip on my jeans and kissing my neck. My body was twisted and a searing pain shot down my leg. 'Adam stop. You're hurting me.'

He let me go and sat up. I got up from the sofa, wanting to tell him it was over, but I couldn't. Our eyes were locked in a battle of wills, both afraid of what each other might say.

'I'm sorry, Susie. Please, don't be angry with me. Please.' His eyes were glassy and I could see he meant what he said.

'Only a few hours ago, you said you would never hurt me. What's got into you?'

'I don't know. I - I just want you to love me.'

I felt close to tears. This wasn't what I'd expected or wanted. 'If you do, you're going about it the wrong way.'

He got up and put his arms round me. We stood holding each other for some time before he said, 'Let's go to bed.'

We went upstairs and didn't speak until we were lying next to each other. He reached over and stroked my face. 'You haven't said you'll forgive me.'

'I forgive you.' The words sounded flat, but I was too tired to say anything else.

He moved over towards me and started to kiss me gently. We made love. It was tender and passionate. By the morning, our row had been forgotten.

Chapter 11

A bundle of letters, held together by a rubber band, dropped onto the doormat. I took them into the study and opened them. Almost all of them contained orders for my relishes. There were forty-five for the asparagus and orange, and ten for the cucumber and red pepper. It was hard to take in. I hadn't expected a response so soon.

I wasn't seeing Adam again until the end of the week, so I had time to buy the ingredients and make what was needed. I wanted some time to myself. Even though we'd made up after our argument, I thought it would help to spend some time apart. A side to his character had emerged that concerned me. He had become increasingly demanding and seemed to expect more from me than I could give. He wanted everything to happen quickly and I wanted to take things slowly. I wondered if we were a good match. You and I had known straight away that we were meant for each other, there were no doubts and no conflicts, especially at the beginning.

He said he was in love with me and I didn't respond. After that, his behaviour changed and he became moody and aggressive. Then he forced himself on me. Perhaps that was when I should have ended the relationship, but something stopped me. Sexually we were very compatible and I needed him.

I couldn't wait to tell Peter about my success at the fair and also find out why he didn't come over to talk to me. Ali's reaction was unnerving, but if she was right, any desire he had for me was bound to surface sooner or later. I tried to compare him with Adam but they were entirely different characters. Peter was calm and introspective while Adam was the opposite. I thought back to the time I'd wanted Peter but now it seemed ludicrous. He wasn't my type at all, but there was something attractive about him in an elusive way. He seemed unobtainable, which made me want to try to win him over. I thought about flirting with him to see what would happen, but then realised that if he didn't want to get involved with me, he would leave and if he did, there would be difficulties with Adam.

Peter had already arrived by the time I got back from the supermarket and was about to start trimming the hedge that ran alongside the road, so I just waved to him from the conservatory. He waved back then carried on with what he was doing.

I watched him sweep the hedge cutter across the top of the hedge with one long graceful movement. It looked effortless. Suddenly he stopped and turned round as if he knew he was being watched. His expression was the same as when he stared at me from the beer tent. I turned away and went into the kitchen.

Now that I knew how to make my relishes, it seemed easy. The most tedious part was preparing and chopping the vegetables, but having the radio on in the background made it feel therapeutic. Once everything was simmering, I went into the sitting room. I hadn't given much thought to marketing and wondered whether I should try publicising my relishes in some local magazines. There were always features on food, and having worked in public relations in the past, it wouldn't be a problem. Maybe I should write about my success at the fair, but I'd need some photos – perhaps Peter could take some? I made a mental note to ask him before he went home.

The delicious smell coming from the kitchen indicated that my relishes were ready. I gave them a stir then took them off the stove.

The noise of the hedge cutter was getting louder. I looked through to the garden and saw Peter trimming the last few feet near the conservatory. The hedge looked immaculate. A few minutes later there was silence. It seemed like a good time to talk to him.

As I approached, he turned round and smiled at me. 'What do you think?'

'You've done an excellent job. Thanks. By the way, did I see you at the fair the other day?'

His smile vanished. 'I did pop in briefly, just to see how things were going. There was a good crowd.'

'Yes, I would imagine Beth raised quite a lot of money. I sold all my relishes.'

'Well done, that's marvellous.' He looked genuinely pleased.

'Why didn't you come over to talk to me?'

'You looked busy. I didn't want to bother you.' He sounded as if he was making an excuse. At the time I saw him, there was no-one at my stall, apart from Adam who came over to chat to me whenever he didn't have customers. I then realised it was probably Adam he was referring to.

'Changing the subject – how's your photography? I need someone to take some photos of me to send with an article to the local press.'

'Actually, I'm pretty good.'

I went into the house to find my camera. I showed him how it worked and we agreed that the next time he came, he could spend half his time gardening and the other half taking photos. He said he'd look forward to it. Ali's comment about him stalking me seemed ridiculous.

By the end of the afternoon I'd bottled sixty jars of the asparagus relish. I'd made a surplus just in case I received more orders. There was still the labelling to do, but that could wait until tomorrow. I'd sold seventy jars at the fair, making a total of two hundred and ten pounds and was due to give half to Beth, so I called her.

'Why don't you come and have supper with us? I've just made a casserole that would feed an army. You can come as soon as you're ready.'

'Thanks Beth, I'd love to.' It was six o'clock. There had been no news from Adam, but, having asked for space, there would be no reason for him to contact me. I went

96

upstairs to change and lay on the bed for a while. I was missing him. I checked my mobile but there were no messages. I tried to imagine what he'd be doing – probably still working. We'd arranged to spend the weekend together which seemed a long way off, but it would be worth the wait. My stomach churned with excitement at the thought of seeing him again, but then I thought of how he tried to force himself on me and how much it had upset me. I took a shower and got ready to go to Beth's.

The walk did me good. It wasn't far but there were two hills between our houses and when I arrived, I felt famished. Beth heard me coming through the gate and opened the door.

'It's lovely to see you. How are you?' She kissed me and showed me into the sitting room. Steve was sitting next to the fire reading, and when he saw me he put down his book and took off his glasses. He offered me a glass of wine.

The room was in its usual state of untidiness, with books and files cluttering the tables. The large sofa had seen better days with all the cushions sinking in the middle, but a colourful throw made it look cosy and comfortable.

'I'm dying to know how much you raised, Beth.'

Her eyes were sparkling with excitement. 'Well, I haven't had everyone's donations yet, but the figure so far is seven thousand five hundred and eighty pounds.'

'That's fantastic. Here's my contribution.' I handed her an envelope with one hundred and five pounds written on the front.

'Thank you my love. That's marvellous. I hear your sex-enhancing relish went down well.'

I told her about the orders I'd received. She asked if I knew how much Adam had raised, and I said probably in the region of two hundred pounds.

'You looked as though you were getting on very well.'

'Yes, it was fun,' I replied, trying to avoid talking about our relationship. Fortunately Steve came back with our

97

drinks and handed me a large glass of white wine. I took a mouthful and gazed into the fire. Beth got up to go into the kitchen. 'I'll just see if everything's ready.'

I offered to help but she told me to relax. She had so much energy I couldn't help admiring her. She also had a good heart and I could see how much Steve adored her. His eyes followed her as she left the room. He was a quiet, hardworking man who loved being outdoors and looking after the garden. The only time he opened up was after a few drinks. At first, I didn't know what to say but then I remembered he liked jazz so we chatted about the band at the fair and then his favourite musicians. We were discussing Scott Joplin when Beth called out that dinner was ready so we went into the kitchen.

A big pot of beef stew sat in the middle of a large, rustic pine table which was surrounded by an odd combination of eight chairs. Some were painted and some were plain, but the different styles seemed to work and added to the eclectic style of the kitchen with its vast array of ornaments, stacks of cookery books and assorted utensils hanging from a rack above the stove. It was more cluttered than the living room.

The smell of the stew made my mouth water. Beth pushed it towards me and I ladled some onto my plate then helped myself to a chunk of homemade bread. Steve topped up our glasses and sat at the end of the table. He tucked into his food while Beth and I talked about the fair. It had gone so well she thought she would organise something else, possibly a barn dance and asked if Adam and I could help by running a raffle. Her inclusion of Adam seemed deliberate as if she was trying to provoke a reaction from me.

'Of course I'll help, but I can't speak for Adam. He doesn't have much spare time. I'll ask him and let you know.' My response prompted her to ask how we were getting on. I told her I was very fond of him, which was all she really wanted to hear. They were good friends and she had seen his marriage fall apart. I wondered if he had told her what he felt for me. Having started the conversation about Adam, I asked what his ex-wife had been like. Beth frowned and said he had doted on her, given her everything she wanted and she had cheated on him. 'She was selfish and ungrateful.'

I'd touched on a sore subject and tried to steer the conversation back to fundraising, but Beth had got the bit between her teeth and carried on.

'It was because Adam worked all hours that God sent. He worked weekends too so she felt neglected. She went off with her boss, a lawyer, called Geoffrey Bates. They'd been having an affair for two years. It was devastating for Adam.'

Steve suddenly looked up. 'No-one knows what goes on in a marriage.'

She was about to reply but changed her mind. 'But then it hasn't been easy for you either, love, has it? I'm sorry,' she said putting her hand briefly on mine.

'It's okay. Things are much better now.'

'Yes, I'm so pleased you've met Adam. He'll make you happy, I know he will.' Her voice resumed its softness and the subject was dropped. Steve excused himself from the table and went back into the sitting room. I then remembered the jar of relish I'd brought with me.

'I thought you and Steve might like to try this. I made it today.' I put the jar on the table so that the word 'aphrodisiac' was facing her. She picked it up, took off the lid and held it up to her nose.

'Smells good and might even do some good.' We both laughed.

'I'm about to do some marketing, so any endorsements would be appreciated.'

Beth promised to give me her honest opinion. I thanked her for supper and as I passed the sitting room, said goodnight to Steve but he had fallen asleep with his book resting on his chest.

I walked back in the moonlight. It was a clear night and the sky was studded with stars. I listened to my footsteps and the occasional rustle of mice going about their nocturnal activities. It was eerily beautiful and I noticed I had cast a faint shadow on the road. An owl flew silently overhead looking for food then landed in a nearby tree. Its sudden screech echoed into the night.

I opened the back door and turned on the light. It was only nine-thirty so I made a mug of hot chocolate and took it into the sitting room. The house felt warm, even though the fire had gone out. I tried to revive it, but without even a spark it was hopeless so I gave up and sat in an armchair.

Beth's comment about Adam was reassuring and I valued her opinion, but Peter's warning still plagued me. I wanted to ask him what he meant but I knew the conversation would end badly. My relationship with Adam was none of his business. I wished he hadn't said anything. Before I went to bed, I checked my emails. There were no new messages.

Offering a postal service had been a bad idea. It took nearly all morning to individually pack and address my relishes. I needed to find retail outlets for them. I also thought that focusing solely on the aphrodisiac aspect would make them more marketable. That afternoon I tried out asparagus with red pepper and asparagus with tomato, both flavours worked well. The next few days were taken up with making and labelling fifty of each flavour, and after finding several farm shops and delicatessens within a reasonable distance, I was ready to see if Rosie's Remarkable Relishes™ would appeal to a wider public.

The week had flown by and I couldn't wait to tell Adam about my new ideas. It was late afternoon and only two hours before he was due to pick me up when a text message arrived. He'd booked us into a hotel for the weekend and I needed to pack a bag with smart and casual clothes. The location was a secret but all would be revealed. He had missed me more than he could say. My heart pounded with excitement as I rushed upstairs to get ready. It had been nearly two years since I'd been away.

I heard his car pull up and opened the front door. He got out and smiled, looking irresistibly handsome. He was wearing a dark blue jacket over a denim shirt and beige jeans, and his hair had been cut short and brushed back so that it stood up. His schoolboy parting had gone. He came into the house and closed the door before taking me in his arms and kissing me. 'I've missed you so much.' We both knew that if we hadn't been going away, we would have gone to bed and made love.

Adam took my bag and put it in the boot of the car. 'So you're taking me on a mystery tour.'

He nodded. 'I think you'll approve of where we're going.'

I stretched over and kissed him on the cheek then sat back in my seat, feeling contented. We headed west along the main road then onto the motorway. 'Well at least I know it's in a westerly direction. Is it by the sea?'

Adam refused to tell me, but he did say we would get there by eight o'clock. It had to be Cornwall. I felt like an excited child. You and I never did anything like this, it was fun. I put my hand on Adam's knee and from time to time, he took his hand off the steering wheel to hold it. I was beginning to feel closer to him and could feel myself letting go. The past was fading and I was rebuilding my life with someone new; someone I could love, but not in the same way as you. I put Peter's warning out of my mind and thought about what Beth had said: 'he'll make you happy, I know he will.'

It was getting dark and there were fewer cars on the road. We turned off the motorway onto the A30 and Adam put on a James Taylor CD. We began to reminisce about our youth and he confessed to having long, wavy brown hair and wearing a head band.

'I suppose you wore a psychedelic kaftan over a pair of flares as well,' I said, laughing. I told him about my passion for buying old curtains from jumble sales and turning them into long dresses. My favourite was made from a thick, gold material and laced up at the front. It was

101

heavy and uncomfortable to wear, but my friends thought it looked very 'hip.' He gave me a sideways glance and shook his head.

We talked about going to the first Glastonbury festival and dancing barefoot to Al Stewart in a smoky haze infused with cannabis and incense. We both agreed it had been worth the lack of sleep but neither of us had wanted to repeat the experience.

Even though it was dark, it was possible to see that the landscape had become more rugged. Gnarled, wind-blown trees were picked out by the headlights and the narrow roads were now lined either side by dry stone walls. We drove on for another half an hour and then slowed down and turned right. After a few minutes we turned left between two imposing stone pillars bearing the name Marston Hall. Solar lights illuminated the long, sweeping driveway which led to a grand, old ivy-covered house. The reception area was calm and welcoming with several guests lounging on large, comfortable sofas in front of an open fire enjoying a pre-dinner drink.

We were given the keys to room thirty-six and took the lift to the second floor. Adam opened the door, put our bags on the floor then led me over to the large, sumptuous bed. There was hardly any time to take in the luxurious surroundings. We swiftly undressed and were soon lost in each other's bodies until we were fulfilled. Afterwards Adam stroked my hair and told me he loved me. I said I loved him too, but the words came out almost without thinking. They sounded stilted and insincere.

We showered and got ready for dinner. I opened the French doors and went out onto a balcony to listen to the sea beyond the large landscaped garden. Adam slid his arms round my waist. 'Is this romantic enough for you?'

I nestled my head against his. 'Perfect. Thank you.' The sea was shimmering like a sheet of silver and the air was still.

By the time we went down for dinner, the dining room was almost empty but we were shown to a table in an alcove and Adam ordered a bottle of champagne. The food, like the surroundings, was superb and by the end of the evening, we were ready for a good night's sleep.

As we walked back to the lift, a couple sitting by the fire caught Adam's attention and he seemed to freeze. The woman was well-dressed with short brown hair and the man was balding and wearing a suit. They were having a nightcap and laughing about something. Adam pulled me towards the stairs. 'I can't believe it. That's Jane, my ex, and her new husband – bloody hell. This could be a disaster Susie. I think we'll have to go somewhere else.' His anger mounted as he ran up to the room, leaving me behind. When I opened the door, he was sitting on the bed with his face in his hands. I tried to console him but he pushed me away. 'I'm so sorry. I wanted to make up for everything.'

'We'll check out in the morning. It'll be okay.'

'I just couldn't face her. I hope you understand.'

We were both feeling exhausted from the journey and too much wine. I put my arms round him and kissed him but he didn't respond so I undressed and got into bed. He got up and stood by the window.

'It's just a dreadful coincidence. Please don't let it spoil our weekend Adam.'

He stared at me, his face like thunder. 'Well, it has.'

He was inconsolable and I didn't know what to say so I turned over and tried to go to sleep. After a while he came to bed but he didn't touch me. 'This isn't my fault. I don't understand why you're taking everything out on me,' I exclaimed.

'You're right, I'm sorry.' He moved over and put his arms round me. It wasn't long before we were making love again, but this time it was rough, almost painful, as if he was thinking about someone else. Afterwards I felt sad, but was overwhelmed by the need to sleep.

The French doors had been left open all night and the voile curtains were lifting in a gentle breeze. Adam was still sleeping. I slipped out of bed and went out onto the balcony. The garden glowed in the early morning sunlight. There were several large oval-shaped yews that ran down either side of the main lawn and in a dip at the bottom was a small lake with a fountain. Beyond that, between some mature trees, was the sea. Directly below, guests were having breakfast in a conservatory. I went back into the room. Adam was awake and sitting up. 'Come here sweetheart.' He held out his arms to me. He seemed to have got over his anger from the night before, but I was hesitant to get back into bed. I sat beside him and he folded his arms around me. I wasn't in the mood for anything more and resisted when he tried to kiss me. 'We'd better get up and have breakfast then get ready to go.'

'Yes, you're right. I don't know what came over me last night. It was such a shock seeing Jane again. I'll feel much better once we're away from here. Let's have breakfast in our room.' Before I could answer, he rang reception. I went into the bathroom and ran a bath.

By ten o'clock we were ready to leave. Adam had told the receptionist we'd received some bad news and needed to return home immediately. Unfortunately we still had to pay the full amount. As we got into the car, I looked back at the hotel thinking how things could have been.

'Where shall we go now?'

Adam suggested going up the coast and finding a bed and breakfast so we drove back the way we came until we reached Port Isaac. He parked the car and we walked down to the town to find a pub for lunch. A strong smell of fish hung in the air and seagulls were scavenging from the brightly coloured fishing boats bobbing up and down in the harbour. It was quaint. I just hoped we would be able to find somewhere to stay. Neither of us had much to say, the disappointment of leaving such a beautiful hotel was still too great.

Lunch was simple in an old pub where the majority of its customers spoke with a Cornish dialect. The tourist season had ended and life had returned to normal. Adam asked the landlord if he could recommend somewhere to stay, but his only suggestion was a small guest house run by his sister, a few doors away. We left and wandered aimlessly through the narrow streets until we both came to the conclusion – we wanted to go home. It was pointless staying in second-rate accommodation just for the sake of spending time away and the weather was gloomy. We headed back to the car and took the coastal route until we reached the main road. Adam turned on the CD player and we continued listening to the gentle voice of James Taylor without saying another word.

It was a relief to be home. I picked up the mail and Adam took the bags upstairs. It was less than twenty-four hours since we set out on our mystery tour and now we were home again. The more I thought about it, the more amusing it seemed. When Adam came back downstairs, we looked at each other and couldn't help laughing.

'Well, I did my best to please you sweetheart, but failed dismally,' he said smiling.

I hugged him and said it was good while it lasted. Later, over dinner, he explained that he and Jane had stayed there once before, but he never thought she'd go back there. Lesson learnt. He'd take me abroad next time, somewhere romantic like Rome or Paris. I wanted him to open up and tell me more about his past. I wanted to get to know everything about him, but he held back. In a way, it was easier for me. The door on my past had closed. There would never be the chance to bump into John again. I was free, Adam wasn't. I wondered if he still loved Jane.

We slept soundly and the next morning, after breakfast, went for a long walk. I told him about the idea of selling my relishes to shops.

'I wish you every success sweetheart. You deserve it.'

We were standing on a hill above the house. The wind was cold so we put our arms round each other and I rested my head against Adam's chest. I'd done the same with you in the past, looking down the valley and thinking how lucky we were. Just for a moment, one fleeting moment, I was with you again.

Chapter 12

Adam left early Monday morning and promised to call me when he got home from work. The weekend had started on a high and thankfully ended on a high. I could still picture Jane. She was slim, attractive and elegantly dressed, unlike her husband who was unattractive, balding and wearing an ill-fitting suit because he was overweight. It was hard to understand what she saw in him.

I wondered what would have happened if they'd seen us. Adam had a short fuse and things could easily have got out of hand. The thought of him and Geoffrey brawling on the carpet made me cringe with embarrassment. We'd had a lucky escape and I was glad we came home when we did.

I decided that I didn't like Jane, not because I resented her, but because she'd hurt Adam so much. Beth said he doted on her and she didn't appreciate it. He'd undoubtedly suffered as a result of the divorce and I felt he didn't trust me. Deep down, he was kind and very loving. He just needed to stop feeling so angry and insecure. I knew it was wrong to compare him with you, but I couldn't help it. You were rarely angry with me and certainly never hurt me. Perhaps, in time, I could make him feel loved again.

The prospect of trying to sell my relishes to shops was nerve-wrecking. I'd never sold anything to anyone before, apart from putting adverts in the 'for sale' columns of local newspapers and running the stall at Beth's charity fair, but I needed to do more to get my business off the ground. At first, I thought of phoning around, but if anyone said 'no,' the opportunity to show them my products would be lost – they needed to be sold face to face.

I'd packed my relishes in boxes of twelve so that small quantities could be bought without too much outlay. I'd also produced more leaflets but removed the order forms. It was time to go knocking on a few doors. I loaded the boxes into the back of my car and drove to a farm shop called Green's four miles away. The name reflected its organic and eco-friendly credentials with most of the products being locally sourced. Everything appeared to be high quality. It seemed like a good place to start.

The shop wasn't busy when I arrived and there was only one assistant behind the counter who was, unsurprisingly, dressed all in green. I asked to see the manager and she disappeared through a door, leaving no-one in charge. The shop was filled with a colourful and interesting range of food, including seasonal fruit and vegetables, but I couldn't see where the preserves were kept. A few minutes later she came back with a young, dark-haired man who introduced himself as Giles. He said he owned the shop and asked how he could help. I produced a jar of relish from my shoulder bag and let him see it from the front then, as I told him about the ingredients, turned it round so he could see the word 'aphrodisiac.' He took the jar from me to look at it more closely.

'This looks interesting. Can I try some?'

He opened the jar and, after smelling the contents, asked me to follow him. We went through the door behind the counter and into his office which also appeared to be a store room. His desk was surrounded by boxes of biscuits, teas, cereals and a variety of other foods. It looked disorganised and I wondered how he managed to work in such chaos. He moved a few of the boxes from a chair and asked me to sit down while he looked for a packet of crackers.

'Would you like a coffee?' He went over to where a kettle and a few mugs were sitting on a worktop next to a small sink. I politely declined and waited while he found a spoon and plate. He wanted to know how I came up with the idea so I told him about Peter and his knowledge of herbs and their medicinal properties, and how one thing led to another. He was fascinated by the claim that asparagus boiled in wine was an aphrodisiac and asked if I'd put it to the test. He grinned. I felt myself blush as I tried to explain that Mr Culpeper *believed* it to be an aphrodisiac. There was no actual proof that it was.

Giles spooned some relish onto a cracker and put it into his mouth. His brown eyes widened and he nodded. 'It's good, really good. Yes, I'd like to give it a try.'

I told him they'd sold for three pounds a jar at a charity fair. We negotiated a thirty per cent discount and he made out a cheque for the cost of twelve. I'd made my first sale and couldn't believe how easy it had been. When I got back to my car, I felt elated. If selling my relishes was going to be this effortless, it would be a very satisfying day. I sent a text to tell Adam the good news. He replied almost immediately saying, 'well done – I'm so pleased for you.'

The next shop on my list was a delicatessen in the small, market town of Westford three miles north. Unlike Green's, it was well-established and had been trading for over twenty years. It was called Food For Thought and focused on fine cheeses, cold meats, homemade pies, chocolates, a few good wines and preserves. The shop front had a 1930s look about it with the name painted in gold italic lettering on a dark brown background. Its window displays were always interesting and usually carried a theme, like the best of Britain, France or Italy. As I approached, I saw the French flag hanging above some patés, cold meats and cheeses next to a basket filled with bread and wine. Everything was neatly arranged on a blue-and-white checked table cloth.

Inside the shop several people were waiting to be served. It didn't seem a convenient time to try out my sales pitch, so I took a quick look around then went to a nearby café for a much-needed cup of coffee and a bite to eat. I decided to leave the delicatessen until last.

The other two shops were similar to Green's but only one called The Market wanted to try my relishes. The owner of the other one said he was going through difficult times and thinking of selling up.

It was late afternoon before I went back to Food For Thought and the shop was empty. A woman with shoulder-length grey hair and thick-rimmed, black glasses was stocking the shelves and when I asked her if I could speak to the owner, she glared at me as if she'd been insulted.

'I own the shop. What can I do for you?'

Her brusque manner threw me and I knew I was wasting my time, but I went through my sales pitch and held up the jar of relish so that she could read the labels. She snatched it from me and turned it round and round.

'What a ridiculous idea. How can a relish be an aphrodisiac? Sorry, I'm not interested.'

I left the shop vowing never to go there again. It was a disappointing end to a good day but I'd made a start and there were bound to be ups and downs.

That evening Adam called. He wanted to see me but I told him I had work to do. He let out a disappointed 'oh,' then said he'd see me tomorrow. It had been a long day and I felt tired, but there was now so much to think about. The next step was coming up with ideas for an article. I sat down at the kitchen table and turned on my laptop. Words came and went. It was late and I was hungry so I made some toast and a cup of tea. The page on the screen remained blank, apart from the word 'saucy.'

The next day, my story took shape. It focused on the relish's unusual health benefits and what had inspired me to create it. I chose not to mention Peter by name and just referred to him as a friend to avoid any unwanted publicity. He was such a private person I didn't think he'd appreciate it. The article ended with where it could be bought and my contact details. All I needed to do was come up with an eye-catching headline and wait for Peter to take some photos which would be the day after tomorrow. My excitement, however, was mixed with trepidation. What if my story created more interest than I could cope with? Perhaps I could ask Beth and a few of her friends to help me. The thought made me anxious, but anything was possible. It was while I was ruminating over the future that the phone rang.

'Hi, is that Susie? It's Giles from Green's. Just thought I'd let you know that I've run out of your relishes. Eight jars sold yesterday afternoon and four this morning, so I'd like to order four more boxes, please.'

'Yes, of course. Would Friday be okay for delivery? I need to make a fresh batch.'

He looked forward to seeing me and put the phone down. The reality of running a business was beginning to sink in and I needed to seek professional advice, especially on financial matters. It would be impractical to keep asking for payment on delivery.

The afternoon was spent shopping and making more relishes. It was early evening before I'd filled the last jar. The kitchen was a mess and the thought of cooking dinner was out of the question. I'd just managed to clear up before Adam arrived, but I was still wearing an apron and there was something sticky on the bottom of my slipper. We kissed and I told him to help himself to a drink while I went upstairs to change. I left my slippers on the doormat.

Adam had picked up my story and was reading it when I came back.

'This will cause a stir.'

'What do you mean?'

'Lady launches saucy new relish….'

'It's meant to create interest, otherwise there's no point. Things seem to be going well anyway. I've just had another order from Green's who sold out within two days.'

He looked surprised. 'That's amazing. I'm delighted for you sweetheart. You deserve a big hug. Come here.'

I sat down and snuggled up against him, which led to kissing and the possibility of not going out at all. 'We'd better get going before the pub stops serving food.'

Before Peter arrived I set up a display of relishes on the

kitchen table. I had several ideas on how they should be photographed. There would also need to be some shots of me holding a jar and looking pleased with myself. The backdrop was very apt with saucepans hanging over the Aga and my collection of pottery on the shelf above. It looked like a well-used and much-loved country kitchen.

I'd put on extra make-up and styled my hair so I looked my best. It all seemed so contrived, but I had to create the right impression. No-one wants to see food being produced in an untidy environment by a dishevelled cook.

Peter arrived early, but before he had a chance to knock on the back door, I opened it and invited him in. He was pleased to see that everything was prepared and liked my arrangement of the jars. He also said I looked nice. It was the first time he'd complimented me in that way and I didn't know how to respond. I changed the subject and told him that I'd managed to sell my relishes to a few shops which made him smile.

'This is just the beginning, Susie. I think you're going to be very successful.'

His comments always surprised me. They seemed to have foresight, as if he knew what was going to happen to me.

'How do you know?'

He studied me with his deep, brown eyes. 'I just know, that's all.' He then walked around the table looking at the display from different angles and stopped at where he said was the right spot. I went over to see what he meant, but couldn't agree. The lighting was poor and the labels difficult to read. 'Don't worry, it'll be fine, you'll see.'

I took his word for it and handed him the camera. He took a few portrait shots, leaning in towards the display then standing back and crouching down. He seemed to know what he was doing and I was impressed. He then told me where to stand and to hold one of the jars up in front of me. His instructions came quickly, telling me to turn towards him then stand sideways and just turn my head towards the camera, then face him again. I felt as

112

though I was at a professional photo shoot.

After a while, he said, 'That's it. I think you'll be pleased with those.' He handed me the camera and stood with his arms folded, waiting to hear my opinion. I couldn't believe what I saw. The quality was stunning. Each picture seemed to have a shaft of light falling on the jar which made the name stand out and the glass shine. I looked at the window but there was only natural daylight and no sun. The ones of me were exceptional too. I was delighted and lost for words.

'Well, what do you think?' Peter looked concerned, as if he thought I was disappointed.

'I don't know how you managed to take such high-quality photos with such a cheap camera, but you have. They're amazing. Thank you.'

He came over to see for himself and stood close to me. I set the camera to slide show and gave it to him. It looked so small in his strong hands.

'I think they should do the job, don't you? I'd better get on with some gardening now.' He put the camera on the table and let himself out of the back door.

I had to look at the pictures again. Peter intrigued me. He was so unassuming yet so talented.

I went into the study and downloaded them onto my computer. They looked even better on a large screen. The rest of the morning was spent selecting the best ones and writing captions for them. By lunch time I was ready to send out my article. I went to look for Peter but he'd already gone.

After sending my story to two local newspapers and three magazines, I got ready to go over to Adam's. He'd promised to cook something which would need an accompaniment. We planned to put my relish to the test, although I wasn't sure how we would tell if it worked or not. Our sex life didn't need improving.

When I arrived, he was taking a ham out of the oven. It had been baking slowly for four hours and was cooked to perfection. He left it to cool and I helped lay the table, putting a jar of my asparagus and orange relish next to the salt and pepper. We then went into the sitting room and opened a bottle of wine.

'Peter took some photos of me with my relishes this morning. They were really good. I've sent the best ones with my story to The Gazette and The County News which come out on Friday. It'll be interesting to see what happens.'

Adam said he'd make a point of buying them. I also told him I'd sent my story to The County Life, The Dorset Vale and Best of The West. It was always more difficult to get interest from magazines but there was a chance they might run a feature on new food producers. I'd have to wait and see. If there was any interest, they would contact me.

We took our wine through to the kitchen and I sat down while Adam served dinner. He loved cooking and it showed. His food was always perfectly presented. I watched him carve the ham which was so tender it fell onto my plate in one huge, delicious slice. We added some relish and started to eat. The combination worked well and I made a mental note for future reference. Adam poured more wine into our glasses and it occurred to me that the effect of the wine might dilute the effect of the relish which made our test rather pointless. We both felt drowsy and by the time we'd cleared everything away, were almost too tired to talk.

'Well, are you feeling anything?' I asked.

We were sitting together on the sofa and Adam looked half asleep. 'Not at the moment but maybe when we go to bed, I'll perk up a bit.'

The test had failed, but to me it was just a piece of folklore – an old remedy passed on from the 19th century, although the man who came up with the idea was renowned for his knowledge of herbal medicines. There had to be an element of truth in it. That night our lovemaking was as pleasurable as ever but nothing extraordinary.

114

It was mid-morning before I got home. My mobile had been switched off and when I turned it on again, I noticed I'd missed six calls. Before I had time to make a coffee, the phone rang again. It was a reporter from The Gazette who wanted to clarify a few points on my story before it was published. He asked if I could substantiate my claim that my relishes were an aphrodisiac. I told him to read my press release again. I'd made it quite clear that the ingredients were *believed* to have sex-enhancing properties. I wasn't stating a fact and anyway, it was Mr Culpeper's belief, not mine. I now realised I could have set myself up for a fall. If the aphrodisiac aspect was derided in any way, it would be a disaster. My business would be destroyed before it had even got off the ground.

It wasn't long before the reporter from The County News called with the same question and I repeated what I'd already said. My heart was pounding and I felt sick. The cynical tone of his voice told me what angle he planned to take.

I made a coffee and slumped down into an armchair. I tried calling Ali but she wasn't at her desk so I left a message for her to call me back.

I'd been a reporter myself many years ago and should have known what might happen. How could I have been so stupid? There was no point in dwelling on what now looked like the inevitable so I put on my jacket and walking boots and headed down to my place of refuge by the river.

I climbed over the stile and walked slowly through the field. The views and fresh air helped clear my mind and I tried to focus on the here and now. It was something you'd taught me to do when everything got too much.

When I reached my favourite spot, I lay down in the long grass. The sky was a dull grey, reflecting my mood. I tried to think of the now but my mind was clouded by the future which I knew would be determined on Friday.

Ali still hadn't returned my call so I sent an email from my phone. A couple of minutes later, there was an 'out of office' reply. Her return date was over a week away, so she must have gone on holiday. I wondered if she was with David. We seemed to communicate less and less these days; our lives had changed so much in the space of a few months. I missed her friendship and having her around. We were always there for each other, but now things were different. She had fallen in love and I felt forsaken and lonely, but not in the same way as I did after losing you. That was an indescribable emptiness, a vacuum that was impossible to fill.

I thought back to when I first saw Peter. It was spring and I had fallen asleep in almost exactly the same place. Now it was almost winter and hard to remember the unbearable grief that I felt then, but I recalled how hopeful he made me feel after our brief conversation. He seemed to put me at ease. Since then we'd become good friends but it was through him that I was now in my current predicament. Then his words 'you're going to be very successful' came back to me. If that was true, I had nothing to worry about. I held onto that thought and stared up at the sky. The clouds were beginning to separate and expose small patches of blue. Something was moving, drifting gently down towards me. It was a small, pure white feather. I watched as it landed softly on my leg then picked it up. The delicate fronds came from a tiny point at the base. Somehow it didn't look like a bird's feather, but it must have been – there was no other explanation. I put it carefully in my pocket and thought about you as I walked slowly home.

When I got back, my anxiety had disappeared. I felt positive and ready to face the consequences of Friday, whatever they might be. I put the feather in the egg cup with the others I'd found and thought about calling Adam, but changed my mind. He hadn't called me so I assumed he was working late and anyway it felt good to spend some time alone. I liked the relaxed nature of our relationship. We saw each other when we felt like it which seemed to suit us both. I then wondered what might happen if the publicity on Friday was positive and I was rushed off my feet. The solution entered my head almost immediately – it was obvious, Adam liked cooking, he could help me. The next time we saw each other I would ask him.

When Friday came, I got up early to go and buy the local newspapers, but just as I was brushing my hair, a text message appeared. Adam had beaten me to it. He'd bought the papers on the way to work and already read the articles. They were just as I'd written them. Nothing had been changed. I sent a quick reply saying thanks for letting me know, but I still had to see for myself. It was too good to be true. He then said he'd be over after work to take me out for dinner. I responded with 'can't wait!'

I drove to the local garage, filled the tank with petrol and picked up copies of both papers. After paying the bill, I walked over to a corner of the shop and quickly flicked through each one until I found my story. They'd even kept the same headline. The relief was overwhelming. The two pictures I'd sent were used and I couldn't help smiling at my attempt to look sexy as I held the jar just above my cleavage. The other picture was a close up of the word aphrodisiac. It was exciting but also frightening to find out what the impact would be. I didn't feel prepared for a surge in orders and began to question my capabilities as a businesswoman. It was still all so new to me.

That afternoon I rang an accountant friend of Beth's who could see me at the end of the day. I'd explained my situation and he was more than happy to help. With so much on my mind, I'd almost forgotten to deliver the order to Green's. It was four o'clock before I set off but there was still enough time to talk to Giles before going on to see the accountant. I wanted to find out if he'd had any customer feedback.

The shop was busy when I arrived and he looked run off his feet. I put the boxes of relish on the counter and waited until he was free. He nodded and smiled at me then held up his hand to say that he'd be five minutes. While I was waiting, I noticed a copy of The Gazette sitting on a shelf behind him. It looked as though it had been read.

When he finally managed to see me, he seemed excited. 'We've had lots of phone calls in response to the newspaper article. I told people that I was waiting for a delivery and to come in tomorrow.'

'That's fantastic. I hope you'll have enough.' I handed him an invoice for payment.

'If not, Susie, I'll order some more.' He took the money from the till and I wrote 'paid with thanks' and the date on the invoice.

'Has anyone said anything about the relish?'

'Yes. A woman thought her husband had become a new man,' he said wryly.

'..No – really? It must be the power of suggestion. That's amazing.' I couldn't help laughing and neither could Giles. He said he'd be in touch as soon as he needed some more and I left the shop, still amused by his comment.

Davis and Sherwood, the accountancy firm, was a ten-minute drive from Green's and I arrived just in time for my appointment with Clive Davis, one of the partners. The receptionist showed me to his office. I'd come with my ideas in my head and hardly anything written down, apart from a record of what I'd spent so far, and the goods I'd sold. I'd already registered Rosie's Remarkable Relishes Ltd as a company name, so at least I was trading legitimately. The newspapers containing my article were tucked under my arm and a jar of relish in my handbag.

Clive shook my hand as he introduced himself and asked me to sit down on the other side of his desk. He was short with receding grey hair but a friendly smile and I warmed to him. Before we got down to business, he asked about Beth and Steve and I told him about her fundraising efforts for the local hospice. I also mentioned how much I'd contributed from the sale of my relishes, which surprised him. We went through my plans and how I intended to develop the business. He then made

118

suggestions and advised how he could help me. We started to talk about marketing and I showed him the newspaper articles which he read with interest.

'I'm sure they will generate a good response, but how will you cope if you have a sudden increase in orders?'

When I said I'd enlist the help of friends, he shook his head. If I intended to work from home, I would need to invest in the right equipment, possibly convert one of the outbuildings and maybe, in time, hire staff. It began to sound like a food factory but he was right. If I wanted my business to be successful, it had to be done the right way. The thought of mass production scared me. I hadn't wanted to run a big enterprise, but nothing was going to happen overnight. By the end of our meeting, I'd agreed to let him manage all my financial matters. It was a huge weight off my mind.

When I got back into the car, I checked my phone. I'd missed eight calls and had six emails from new customers. My head started to spin. The pressure was beginning to mount and I couldn't wait to see Adam. When I got home, his car was already parked next to the house. I parked behind him but his car was empty. It was getting dark so he couldn't have gone for a walk. I went through the gate to see if he was in the garden and noticed him standing some distance away by the fish pond. I called out and ran towards him.

'Oh Adam, I'm so pleased to see you. Everything's gone mad since this morning. I've got lots more orders and don't know if I can cope.'

'Hey Susie, calm down.' I fell into his arms. 'Everything will be okay. You just need to explain that you're a one-man business and there might be a slight delay in fulfilling the orders. I'm sure people will understand.'

'Would you be able to help?'

'Yes, I expect so. Let's go indoors.' He kissed me on the forehead and put his arm round my waist as we walked towards the house.

'What were you doing out here anyway?'

'It wasn't so dark when I got here so I thought I'd have a look at the garden. Then I heard a frog and wandered down to the pond.'

I started to shop online. The quantities of ingredients and other items had rapidly escalated and I needed more production time. My days were now taken up with cooking and evenings with labelling and preparing invoices. Adam helped as much as he could. I'd given him precise cooking instructions to make sure the relishes all tasted the same, but somehow his always tasted better. When I mentioned it, he just put it down to being a better cook.

We spent weekends together as much as possible, but sometimes his veterinary work took precedence. The pressure I was under made me tired which began to take its toll and we would often argue about the most trivial things. Our bickering would usually last until bed time, but by the morning everything had been forgotten.

Enquiries kept coming by phone and email and it soon became clear that I needed to expand. The orders from Green's Farm Shop kept increasing until I was almost at breaking point, so I finally rang Beth to ask if she could help. She didn't hesitate to say yes and said she would ask two of her friends to lend a hand. I felt as though I was fire-fighting, but somehow I managed to fulfil the orders. My turnover was increasing rapidly and Clive suggested borrowing money to convert one of the wooden outbuildings, but I had enough capital of my own and, thanks to Steve and a few of his friends, the renovation work soon got underway. The outbuilding wasn't huge, but it was large enough to accommodate the equipment I now needed and give me back my kitchen which was hardly recognisable. Every available surface was permanently covered with jars, pans, utensils, empty wine bottles and boxes. It had become virtually impossible to move around in. Adam couldn't bear the clutter and his visits grew more infrequent. We both knew it was better for me to get away and spend time at his house, even though his kitchen now resembled mine, but on a much smaller and neater scale. At least we could go for walks along the beach and clear our minds. There was something about the sea's vast emptiness and its slow, undulating movement that was mesmerising. I could watch it for hours and never feel bored. It had so many moods.

We'd just got back to the cottage after a bracing walk. Our faces were red from the cold wind so we were pleased to see the log fire still glowing in the sitting room. I was now conscious of constantly being contacted by customers and tried to ignore my phone, especially on Sundays. Adam had gone upstairs to the bathroom and for some reason, having been alerted to a new message, thought I'd take a look. It was from Sophie Williams who worked for the Best of The West magazine. She wanted to interview me about my relishes.

As Adam came back downstairs, he stopped and said, 'You're looking pleased with yourself, what's happened?'

I told him about the email and he raised his eyebrows. 'That's great, but I won't be able to take on any more work, Susie. Sorry.'

'It's okay, I'll manage somehow. Beth and some of her friends are helping me now and as soon as my outbuilding's ready, I'll have the capacity to produce more myself. I might even take on an assistant.'

'I can't believe how quickly your business has grown in just a few months. I'm so proud of you.' He sat next to me and gave me a hug. He then whispered, 'I do love you Susie Chester.'

Chapter 13

Sophie Williams was keen to interview me at home. She wanted to see where I lived and worked so that she could get a feel for me as a person. In a way, it was a nuisance as I had to reorganise the kitchen and move all the boxes to the study so they could be shut away. I'd got used to having everything to hand and, despite the clutter, had managed perfectly well. I'd been assessed for hygiene and was fastidious about cleanliness, but anyone seeing where I worked for the first time might think otherwise.

Before she arrived, I went to check on Steve's progress with renovating the barn. The building had been reduced to a shell and he and two friends had started recladding it with new planks of timber. The rusty metal roof had been taken off and thrown onto a skip ready to be replaced with a new, non-corrosive one. Steve seemed to have everything under control and I was impressed by what had been achieved in less than a week. I told him to keep up the good work, and when he and his friends were ready, to come and help themselves to some lunch which I'd leave on the garden table.

As I walked back to the house, I tried to think of some answers to questions Sophie might ask me. I didn't want to involve Peter so thought I'd say he was just someone I'd met who knew about the healing properties of herbs. If she wanted to know more about him, I'd say I couldn't help her.

Before I had a chance to think of anything else, there was a knock at the front door. It was Sophie, carrying a camera and voice recorder. She introduced herself and came into the sitting room. Although the cottage was old and characterful, most of my furniture was modern. I liked the contrast, but it wasn't to everyone's taste and I could tell by her expression as she looked around the room that it wasn't hers. She was young, probably in her twenties, with short, blonde hair and inquisitive green eyes which were heavily made up with black eyeliner and brown eye shadow. She sat on the edge of an armchair and seemed nervous which made me feel uneasy. I got the impression she wasn't very experienced and when I asked how long she'd worked for the magazine, she said it was her first job. I had a feeling the interview would not be very long or particularly thorough, but was prepared to reserve judgement until it was over.

I sat on the sofa and watched while she set up her voice recorder on the coffee table. Before she turned it on, she coughed. She began by asking me about my past and how long I'd been widowed. My answer was brief and to the point – I didn't want to dwell on that aspect of my life. The next question was when and how did I come up with the idea for my relishes. Her interview technique wasn't very inspiring. I wanted her to ask more searching questions, but she didn't and I started to feel disheartened. It would have been better if we'd just had a conversation. Time was getting on and I had a lot of work to do. She could see I was getting impatient.

'If you like, I'll show you around. I'm having one of the outbuildings converted into a workspace as I've outgrown the kitchen.'

She picked up her voice recorder and camera. When she saw the kitchen she understood what I meant and took a photo of me standing in a small space between the table and the sink. We chatted generally and she began to relax. I was feeding her information that I thought would make a good story. We then went up to the barn which was now looking more like a building again and Steve and his team posed for a photo. She also took another picture of me with the barn and garden in the background. Afterwards, she said she'd got enough information to write something and would contact me if she needed to know anything else. We went back down to the house and I gave her a jar of my best-selling relish. She asked if it worked and I told her to try it for herself. I also promised to email her some of my pictures, just in case they were needed. She wished me

123

luck and said she'd send me a copy of the magazine when the story was published in a few weeks' time then left by the back door.

Every day brought new enquiries and new orders. I called Beth to see if she could help with another batch but she sounded tired and I apologised for asking. She said she didn't mind but was tied up with other things and gave me the phone number of her friend Clare Richardson who was looking for part-time work. I called her straight away and explained my situation. She was happy to help so I said I'd call in to see her after I'd made some deliveries later that day.

Green's was still my best customer, but The Market and three other delicatessens were now placing regular orders. Until I had the ability to produce larger quantities, they had to make do with what I could generate on a weekly basis which was around sixty jars per shop. Adam fluctuated between wanting to help then not wanting to and made me feel guilty for asking.

Fiona Harmsworth, who ran The Market, was a bundle of energy and a great character. She seemed to be able to deal with half a dozen things at once and was always pleased to see me. In many ways, she reminded me of Ali, but on a more boisterous scale. We hit it off as soon as we met. The Market was my last delivery of the day and when I walked in, she was putting some cucumbers into a willow basket.

'It's the lady with the raunchy relishes – lovely to see you.'

I asked where she wanted them. She took the box from me and put it on the counter. We chatted about business and the impact my relishes were having which seemed to be a continual source of amusement.

'Everyone jokes about sex. It's great fun and gets people talking to each other. My staff can't stop laughing these days and if they're happy, I'm happy.'

'Apart from its entertainment value, has anyone said

they like it?'

'They love it Susie, which is why I keep running out.' She said it was the most sensual food she'd ever eaten. The consistency was soft and delicate but it had a kick that rippled around her body and made her feel warm inside. I thought I'd remember that. It would be good for future publicity.

Clare lived about a mile from me and I wondered why we'd never met before. She lived in a former schoolhouse which must have served the local community before and after the First World War. Although it was small, it had a foreboding appearance, with tall, narrow windows and thick stone walls but the pale blue woodwork made it look more contemporary. A dog barked when I knocked at the front door. She opened it a fraction so that the small Border terrier couldn't escape.

'Hello Clare, I'm Susie.'

'Hi, come in. This is Alfie – I hope you don't mind dogs.' Alfie jumped up at me, barking excitedly.

She ushered me into a large, tastefully furnished square room with a vaulted ceiling. Alfie was led away to another room and shut in. When she came back she apologised on his behalf and sat down opposite me. She was tall and slim with cropped auburn hair and large, almost masculine, features but her voice was soft and feminine. She said her husband worked in London during the week and that she was looking for something to keep her occupied while he wasn't around. She'd had a part-time office job up until a month ago, but was made redundant and now happy to do anything. When I told her I needed someone to initially work from home, she frowned, but her main concern was Alfie and whether he would create a hygiene problem, but I reassured her that as long as he was kept out of the kitchen and her workspace was kept spotlessly clean, everything would be fine.

I asked how she'd got to know Beth and half-expected her to say through charity work, but they'd met at a party just after she and her husband had moved to the area a year ago. She started to say something else then stopped. I waited to see if she'd continue, but she didn't.

'It's okay. You can ask me anything you like.'

'Beth told me you lost your husband last Christmas. I just wanted to say I'm sorry and that it must be really hard for you.'

It had been a long time since anyone had said those words and my mind flashed back to the time just after the funeral. No-one phoned or called round to see me thinking I should be left alone to grieve. How misguided they were. I'd never felt so desperate for company.

'Yes, it's been hard, but I've survived. You just have to get on with life as best you can.' I blinked hard until the tears clouding my eyes disappeared. 'Things are so much better now, thanks to good friends and a rapidly growing business which keeps me on my toes.'

'I'd really like to help you Susie. I'm a good cook. You can ask my husband Tom.'

'I'm sure you are. Maybe I could just take quick look at your kitchen?'

'Yes, of course you can.'

As we walked along the hallway, Alfie started barking from the study and was immediately told to be quiet. Her state-of-the-art kitchen was enormous and immaculately clean. I explained what I wanted her to do and suggested she spent a morning with me so she could see how I worked. We agreed an hourly rate and arranged for her to come over later in the week. It was a relief to know I wouldn't have to ask for Adam's help anymore. When I got home, I called him to let him know. By the end of our conversation, he'd invited himself over. He was missing me. After a light meal and a couple of glasses of wine, we went to bed and made love then fell into a deep sleep. The next morning, I was only half-awake when he left. I remembered him kissing me on the forehead and telling me he loved me before going back to sleep again. When I woke an hour later, I thought it had all been a dream, but then recalled him saying something about Saturday.

Breakfast was eaten while chopping a pile of vegetables. I had two orders to fulfil then collect a new set of labels from the printers. Every day there was always so much to do, and usually no time for reflection, but today was different. In just under two months it would be Christmas. Until now, I hadn't given it much thought, but Clare's comment reminded me that the festive season was drawing closer, and so, inevitably, was the first anniversary of your death. The prospect of pretending to be happy filled me with dread, but it would be expected, particularly from customers. Adam had promised we'd spend Christmas together at his house, which would help, but I knew it wasn't going to be fun. How could it be?

As I slowly stirred the contents of four large saucepans, all the painful memories came flooding back.

It was a cold December night. You were sitting downstairs in an armchair wrapped in a blanket because it was too painful to lie down – then I remembered you curling up and groaning. I rushed to fetch some liquid morphine, which seemed to work for a while. I sat on the arm of the chair and tried to comfort you, holding you against me and gently stroking your hair. You looked up at me and whispered, 'I think it's time for me to go into the hospice Susie – I need more care.' We had reached the point neither of us had wanted to face.

In the morning I packed a small holdall for you with a wash bag, a clean pair of pyjamas, a dressing gown and your brown leather slippers. The hospice had already been notified and my phone call expected.

When we got there, you walked into your room, got undressed and got into bed. A few days later you found it difficult to do anything unaided. Christmas was only four days away so I put up a small, artificial tree on a table and arranged some presents underneath it in the hope that we could spend our last Christmas together. The tree was decorated with lots of tiny red and green baubles. I remembered how you tried to smile and managed to say,

'Love you.' You said you were terrified of dying. I will never forget the desperate look in your eyes.

That night I couldn't sleep. I've never been religious but I prayed with all my heart that you would be taken care of. Early the next morning, the phone rang. A nurse asked me to come as soon as I could. I packed an overnight bag and jumped into my car. I tried to remain calm, but my heart was thumping and a lump formed in my throat, making it difficult to swallow.

When I reached your room, two cleaners were busy mopping the floor and I found it awkward to say anything. You were sitting up in bed and all we could do was look across the room at each other. I gesticulated that I would go and make myself a cup of tea. When I got back, the cleaners had gone and a nurse was sitting next to you holding your hand. She looked up at me. 'He's going now,' she said calmly.

I couldn't believe that I'd lost the chance to talk to you one last time. 'No, no, not now, not so soon,' I pleaded. Your breathing became fast and shallow and your eyes were closed. She stroked your face and said the loving words that I wanted to say, but I was too shocked by what was happening. I had never seen anyone die before. She said you could hear me so I told you how much I loved you and how happy you had made me. Your hand gently squeezed mine and then you stopped breathing.

Tears didn't come until I'd left the room and then I wept. I wept for your suffering, for my loss and to ease the pain of my broken heart. It was over. The battle you had fought so bravely and with so much dignity had been lost. We were not ready to be torn apart in such a devastating way. All I could think was, why? Why death? Why you? Why us? Why? A beautiful light had gone out and I felt so utterly alone.

I took the pans off the stove before breaking down. My body shook as I sobbed. Just the word Christmas had triggered so much pain and I wondered if it would ever go away. As much as I tried to believe that everything was

128

okay, I knew my grief was still bubbling away under the surface ready to erupt like a volcano, but I had too much to do. I had to finish my relishes. I couldn't give in to my emotions like this. After wiping my tears away, I took the sterilised jars out of the oven. My heart was aching but my head told me to focus on my work.

Someone once told me that all of life's negative experiences can be turned into positive ones and I now understood what they meant. The human spirit can endure unimaginable pain and suffering and still overcome it. My grief was nothing in the scheme of things and it had helped me become a stronger person. I had channelled my negative energy into something positive and been rewarded. I also had the love of good friends who I knew I could count on. The adage 'count your blessings' was true. I had a lot to be grateful for and never understood people who were always dissatisfied and wanting what they didn't have. If they looked at what they did have and were thankful for it, they'd easily find contentment.

Ali's invitation to dinner came by email. She and David had been in France and got back two weeks ago, but she'd been frantically busy at work and not had a chance to contact me before now. She thought I'd understand – which I did. She was in love. The dinner party was a week on Saturday. I sent a text to Adam who responded immediately with 'that sounds great' and 'can't wait to see you again sweetheart.' I reciprocated and said I'd be over as soon as I could on Saturday.

Clare was due at ten o'clock. Luckily I'd caught up with all my orders and could take my time showing her the ropes. It wasn't difficult but if she mirrored what I did then the end result would hopefully turn out the same.

Steve and his friends were making good progress with the barn. From the outside it looked finished, apart from staining the wood. Inside was taking shape faster than I anticipated and the need to buy equipment more urgent. I'd already decided on the layout with lots of storage, an industrial size cooker, sink unit, dishwasher, fridge, freezer and a large work space. It was now a case of buying the right products but the choice was extensive and I found it confusing.

Being in an area three times the size of my kitchen felt liberating and the prospect of being able to share my workload with Clare, a great relief. I hoped we'd get on and be able to make light of some of the tedium involved. It was repetitive work so she would need a sense of humour.

She arrived on time and as she walked towards the front door I opened it to let her in. She immediately removed her thick, quilted jacket which I hung up for her. We commented on the cold weather and the chance of rain turning to snow. I offered her something to drink. She said tea would be lovely and sat down by the fire.

When I came back, she was reading the copy of The Gazette containing my article. I put the tray on the coffee table.

'This is amazing. It must have generated a huge response.'

'Yes, it did. I wasn't sure I could cope, but with some help, managed okay.' I asked if she took milk before pouring the tea.

'How many shops do you sell to?'

I gave her the names of my regular customers and how much they ordered each week but then added the few shops that hadn't yet reordered, as well as the one-off orders that came by email.

'Seems business is thriving and in such a short time.'

'It's certainly taken me by surprise.'

The conversation then moved on to people we knew, but apart from Beth and Steve, she hadn't really got to know anyone else. I asked if she'd met a vet called Adam Walker but she shook her head. She said she'd heard of him and that he was known to be a bit of a womaniser. I must have looked shocked. She asked if I knew him.

'Yes, we've met once or twice.' I was determined to

find out more. 'I'm intrigued. Tell me what you've heard about him.'

'I'm sure it's just idle gossip, but he's been known to seduce a number of married women around here. Well, I suppose someone in his profession has the opportunity to do that sort of thing. He's apparently a very attractive man.'

My heart was pounding. 'Yes, he is and I think you're right – it's just gossip. Come on, let's go and make some relishes.' I was due to see Adam tomorrow and felt like cancelling but changed my mind.

It was impossible to concentrate and my anger made me do everything at high speed which meant cutting my thumb, dropping vegetables on the floor and letting the pan boil over. Clare looked bemused. I tried to explain what I was doing and why and then apologised, saying that I was tired and this might have been a bad idea. She sympathised and tried to console me. I gave her the recipe and asked if she could try making some at home then bring it over for me to taste. She nodded and looked as though she regretted her decision to help me. I was too angry to care. She put her jacket back on and left.

It took almost an hour to clear up the mess in the kitchen. Afterwards I checked my emails. There were no new enquiries so I sat down with a strong cup of coffee and mulled over what Clare had said. Rumours are usually based on some truth – they don't just come from nowhere. I didn't anger easily but the thought of Adam having flings with lots of married women made me furious. Then I thought of Beth and how fond she was of both of us. She would never have allowed me to get involved with someone I couldn't trust. Perhaps all this happened before he met me. I wanted to call him but thought it best to wait. We needed to sort this out face-to-face.

The drive to Canford Bay took longer than usual. A tractor pulled out in front of me and my speed was reduced to fifteen miles an hour. It added to the anxiety I already felt.

Each time I tried to overtake, there was a bend ahead and I had to pull in.

I rehearsed what I was going to say to Adam. If the rumours were true, I knew he would lose his temper and our relationship would be over, but the thought of more emotional pain made me feel sick.

The tractor turned off and I put my foot down. Twenty minutes later I turned right into the lane that led to his cottage. He came out to meet me.

'I got worried and was going to call you.' He kissed me on the lips and cuddled me, but I didn't respond.

'I got held up. The traffic was bad. Sorry.'

We went indoors and he poured me a glass of wine. 'This will help you unwind, sweetheart.'

'Thanks.' I sat down.

'I met Clare yesterday.'

'How did you get on?'

'Okay. She seems competent. We talked about people we knew. She said she'd heard about you.'

'Not difficult being a vet.'

'No, she called you a womaniser.'

He frowned and then laughed. 'That's ridiculous. I don't have time for that sort of thing and anyway, I've fallen for you hook, line and sinker.'

'Is that the truth?'

'Yes. Look, a lot of women flirt with me and in the past I've been tempted, especially after Jane left, but that was a long time ago.'

'I want to trust you. There's no point if I can't.'

He took my glass from me and put it on the mantelpiece. 'Come here.' He pulled me up from the sofa and kissed me, as if to convince me, but somehow I knew he was telling the truth. I could see it in his eyes. 'I don't want to lose you,' I said softly.

'Believe me, you won't. You know how I feel about you.'

Even though we'd had our ups and downs, Adam was a good man. I'd expected him to get angry but he hadn't.

132

Whatever he'd done in the past was no longer important. All that mattered was now.

Chapter 14

I didn't think I'd hear from Clare again. Our meeting hadn't gone well. I'd shown myself to be bad-tempered and clumsy and wouldn't have been surprised if she changed her mind about working for me, but she phoned early Monday morning to say she'd made some relishes and wondered if she could bring them over for me to try. I'd received several new orders and had a lot to do so we agreed on a time towards the end of the day. She said she'd see me later.

The morning passed quickly and by lunch time I'd made enough relishes to fulfil two of the orders. The afternoon was split between cooking and helping Steve. The barn was now ready for fitting out and would be finished in less than three weeks.

Before Clare arrived, I wrote a message to Ali to confirm our dinner date. I hadn't seen her since the fair and was looking forward to catching up with her. She said she had something to tell me. I sensed it had something to do with David and wondered if he'd proposed to her. They'd been staying in a villa near Cannes for two weeks which sounded blissful. I told her Adam and I were getting on well and that my business was thriving. After sending the email, I looked at my watch – it was almost five.

Clare was late and apologised. She came in through the back door holding a small box containing four jars of relish which she put on the kitchen table. She told me which ones were which then asked if I'd had a good weekend. I nodded and said it was relaxing and that I was sorry for the way things went the other day. She realised I was under pressure and dismissed it as nothing. I was glad I hadn't upset her.

I opened one of the jars of asparagus and orange relish I'd made earlier and then one of hers and compared the smell. I spooned some of each onto a plate to compare the colour and consistency. It was hard to tell them apart. The taste too seemed identical. I was delighted and congratulated her on being the first person to replicate my relish in almost every way. She looked pleased with herself. I asked her when she would be able to start and she said, 'Whenever you want me to.' We agreed on tomorrow.

I gave her some of the orders I'd received which had to be ready for delivery on Thursday. I said I'd pick them up from her by lunch time. We sorted out the ingredients and put them into two large cardboard boxes. The jars were already packed in cartons of twenty-four so I gave her six and suggested she ran them through the dishwasher before using them. I also gave her some labels. We loaded everything into her car, but before she left, I took her up to the barn to show her where we would soon be working. She was impressed by the space and its scope for expanding the business. I liked her organised and practical approach and felt sure we would get on well once we'd got to know each other better.

After she'd gone, I thought about my weekend with Adam and wondered if I should tell her about our relationship, but then I realised it might embarrass her. After all, she was the person who'd told me about his reputation. The more I thought about it, the more I couldn't understand why she didn't know, especially as Beth liked a bit of gossip now and again.

By Friday, I felt exhausted. Even with Clare's help, I'd worked from early morning until late at night. Adam was picking me up at midday on Saturday so that we could have lunch then go for a walk. He planned to change at my house before going out in the evening.

It was one o'clock. He'd been delayed and by the time he arrived I was famished, so we drove to the Three Horseshoes at Hatch End just a few miles away. I'd always thought of the pub as mine and Ali's local. The last time we were there it was a beautiful, warm day but I remembered how numb I felt. My loss was still so raw. Ali

135

bought me lunch and was trying to console me but nothing could penetrate the black wall that surrounded me, even the sunshine. It was amazing how much my life had changed.

The pub wasn't busy and we sat at a table by the window. A fire smouldered in the inglenook and a thin veil of wood smoke hung in the air. A large ginger cat lay on the hearth and I wondered how it could stand such intense heat. Adam went to the bar to get some drinks and order food. While he was gone, I gazed through the window. Some crows were circling above an ash tree. I watched them fly down and land one by one in the upper branches until they'd disappeared from sight. The sky was grey and looked heavy with rain, but it was too cold. I wondered if it would snow.

Adam came back with a pint of beer and a glass of wine. '…Penny for your thoughts.'

I'd never liked that expression and felt like saying, 'none of your business,' but I just looked at him and said, 'I think it might snow.'

He took a sip of beer. 'I needed that. It's been a hell of a week.'

I agreed and told him about Clare coming to work for me. He wanted to know more about her, so I told him what I knew. When I said she had a pet dog called Alfie, he glared at me.

'Why are you looking at me like that?'

'I don't want to go over old ground, but she came on to me once. I think she'd just moved here and brought Alfie in with an ear infection.' He laughed and said he couldn't believe it, and then he became angry. 'How dare she call me a womaniser – she made it obvious to me what she wanted. I can assure you it wasn't the other way round.'

'It all makes sense. You spurned her advances so she wanted to get her own back. What shall I do? I'm not sure I want her to work for me now.'

'Forget it. She'll be the one to lose face if she sees me again.'

136

'I didn't tell her about us.'

He shook his head and said it was a long time ago so not worth worrying about. I thought about the similarities between Jane and Clare, but I could never understand infidelity. There was no excuse for it – it just seemed so deceitful and wrong.

By the time we'd finished lunch it was almost three o'clock so I suggested driving back to the cottage and going for a walk by the river. The place I shared with you wasn't visible from the main footpath and the track that led to it barely noticeable, so it would always be a secret. Peter must have come across it by chance.

Adam climbed over the stile first then helped me over. As I jumped down he kissed me. His lips felt hot against the cold air and for a moment I wanted him. I knew he felt the same but we let go of each other and walked towards the river. The water looked murky as it flowed past in the dull afternoon light. Everything else was still. It was the time of year when animals and birds seem to disappear. Even the grass had died back into lifeless, matted clumps. We held hands and quickened our pace to keep warm. When we reached the next stile, Adam looked at me and said, 'The light's fading. I think we should go back.'

We hadn't gone very far, but I realised he was right. We got back to the cottage just before dark. Adam made some tea and I went upstairs to run a bath. I added some jasmine oil to the water and was swirling it around with my fingers when he appeared in the doorway. I turned off the taps and looked at him. He held out his hand and I let him lead me into the bedroom.

We undressed and lay close together on the bed. At first, he gently caressed and kissed my breasts and then his hand moved down to stroke the insides of my thighs; his delicate touch making me gasp. He then lifted his muscular body above mine and I pulled him towards me. At first his movements were slow and pleasurable, but as our need for each other grew, he increased their intensity, thrusting deeper and faster until we were consumed and

137

suspended in a wave of ecstasy. Afterwards, we lay still enjoying the warmth of each other until we almost fell asleep.

Ali lived in a new house on a bland estate, close to where she worked. It was practical and suited her but it wasn't the sort of place where I'd choose to live. The last time I'd visited her, I got lost as all the roads looked the same. Fortunately Adam's sense of direction was better than mine and we managed to find it straight away. It had a neat but small front lawn with one flower bed. Ali had never liked gardening. We walked up the drive and knocked on the red front door.

Ali was thrilled to see us and greeted us both with a kiss. She looked tanned, happy and glamorous in a chic, knee-length black dress. Adam said she looked gorgeous and I could see by the way he was looking at her, he meant it. David came out from the kitchen to say hello. I'd forgotten how tall and handsome he was. He took our coats and Ali showed us into the sitting room. David offered us a drink and a few minutes later came back with four glasses of wine.

I sensed Ali was dying to talk to me alone so I asked if I could help her with dinner. Adam and David seemed happy to resume the conversation they'd had a few weeks ago so we went into the kitchen.

'We're both so busy these days, it's hard to find the time to talk to each other, but I wanted to tell you face to face.'

'I think I know. You're getting married.'

'No, David's asked me to live with him.'

'That's wonderful. I'm so pleased for you.' I threw my arms around her and kissed her on the cheek. 'I knew it would be something like that.'

'We had such a wonderful holiday and by the end, didn't want to go our separate ways so decided not to. I can't believe it. I'm so happy. I'll be moving in with him and commuting from Bath. It doesn't take long by train.'

The thought of Ali moving away didn't occur to me. She'd told me David's work allowed him to live anywhere and I'd assumed he would move in with her. A deep pang of sadness hit me and I couldn't help admitting it. 'I'll miss you so much.'

'We'll still see each other. I'm not moving far and you and Adam can come and stay. It'll be great to go to the theatre together.' Ali tried hard to console me.

'Yes, and you can come and stay with me when you want to get away from it all.' My feelings were a mixture of loss and happiness, but mostly loss and Ali could see it.

'Oh, sweet pea, I know how you feel, but we'll never lose touch. We've been through too much together. We'll always be friends.' She stroked my arm and I tried to smile. I told her about my business and said how little time I'd have in the future, but she was right, we'd never lose touch. Life moves on and change is inevitable. Nothing stands still.

I helped her take the starters through to the dining table. Adam and David came and sat down, still talking about climate change. Ali and David kept glancing at each other. I couldn't help thinking how lucky they were. They'd fallen in love and made a commitment to each other. Deep down I knew my future with Adam wouldn't be forever. Although we enjoyed being together, we also liked being apart and somehow I still doubted him. Clare's comment hurt me and even though he'd told me it wasn't true, I kept thinking about it. I watched him as he continued talking to David. Just over an hour ago, we were making love and now I felt almost invisible.

Ali sat next to me and started to tell me about her holiday. My mind was immediately filled with images of sun-kissed beaches, old French villages, wine, delicious food and the smell of lavender. It was where you and I had always spent our summer holidays. We were always drawn back to the same place and got to know it so well, we thought about living there. Perhaps I would go back one day, but not yet. It would still be too painful. I couldn't

139

imagine being there without you.

David refilled our glasses then went to get another bottle of wine. I'd hardly spoken to him and wanted to get to know him. I excused myself from the table and followed him into the kitchen. As I walked in, he turned round and asked if I was okay. I told him I was thirsty and needed some water so he took a glass from the cupboard and filled it up for me.

'How long have you been with Adam?'

'Not long. Probably a bit longer than you've been with Ali.'

'She's told me all about you.'

I knew from the look in his eyes he was referring to my loss. 'I'm sure she has. Well, I don't expect there's much to add, apart from getting my new business venture off the ground.'

'I'm afraid she's told me about that too.' We laughed and went back to the dining table.

Adam was talking to Ali about animal welfare and the increase in cruelty. He gave a few examples of animals he'd recently treated which had suffered horrific injuries. I looked at him and said, 'I think I'm about to lose my appetite.'

He frowned. 'Sorry everyone – didn't mean to put you off your food.'

I helped Ali clear away the starters. Adam was staring at his wine glass. He looked irritated, but David diplomatically changed the subject to the book he'd bought from him at the fair.

Back in the kitchen, Ali asked how I felt about Adam. It was a difficult question to answer because any uncertainty would allow her to say 'I warned you,' so I said I was in love with him but it wasn't the same as my love for John. Before she had a chance to answer, I mentioned what Clare had said and that Adam had strongly denied it. She stared at me. 'Do you believe him?'

'I want to.'

We put the main course on the table and sat down.

Adam and David were laughing about something. Ali looked at me. 'They're getting on well, aren't they?'

I nodded. She put her hand on mine. 'You'll be fine. Your business is doing well and keeps you busy. I think Adam's a great guy and we could all have so much fun together.'

She had always been a good judge of character and I valued her opinion.

'So you think I should believe him?'

'You'd know if he was playing around.'

It was true. My business did take up a lot of my time but Adam was always there when I needed him. We also spent practically every weekend together.

'You're right.' Life was too short to worry about ridiculous rumours. I looked at him and felt bad for doubting him.

The evening continued amiably with all of us trying to put the world's problems to rights. David's knowledge of current affairs was impressive but Adam stood his ground and I felt proud of him.

When it was time to say goodbye, we thanked Ali and David and said how much we'd enjoyed the evening. It had been just like old times. As we walked towards the car, I looked back. They were standing together in the doorway with their arms round each other. My heart sank at the thought of Ali moving away but I knew she would always remain my dearest friend. Before we drove off, I turned round to wave but they had already closed the door.

Chapter 15

It was the run up to Christmas and the demand for my relishes was beginning to overwhelm me. A Christmas gift idea of three jars in a box had taken off beyond my expectations, and I was now looking forward to Christmas Eve and the day itself just to rest.

Clare's enthusiasm and commitment had taken me by surprise and when I asked if she could increase her hours from three mornings to three days a week, she jumped at the chance. At first, I hadn't known how to take her. I was still smarting from her attempt to flirt with Adam. The thought entered my head almost every time I looked at her but she was proving to be a great asset, so I decided to forget about it. We were becoming good friends.

Peter told me he was taking a holiday and wouldn't be back until the new year. He'd repaired some fencing and cut down some branches from a dying ash tree which he'd chopped into logs. I gave him some extra money, a good bottle of wine and a few jars of relish, and he gave me a small gift wrapped in gold paper. I hadn't expected anything from him so it was a lovely surprise. We wished each other happy Christmas and I kissed him on the cheek. He smiled then touched my shoulder which made it tingle. I told him he had healing hands. He laughed and shook his head as he walked through the gate.

Not having him around felt strange. I looked down at the small box and opened the label. It read, 'Love bears all things; believes all things; endures all things. Love never ends. To my dearest Susie, thinking of you this Christmas. Yours Peter.' The spot where he'd touched me was still tingling and made me feel warm inside. I read the label again and thought of you. The anniversary of your death was approaching and I planned to have the day to myself so that I could plant a Christmas rose by your grave. Its soft white flowers and dark green leaves were a joy to behold and that was how I always wanted to remember you.

Clare's sudden appearance interrupted my thoughts.

'Are you okay, Susie?'

'Yes. Sorry, I was miles away. Peter's just left. He gave me a present.' I showed her the box. She looked at me curiously then said Giles had just phoned. He wondered when he might get his delivery and if I could bring it over personally.

'I'll call him back. I'm just going down to the cottage. I won't be long.' As I walked through the back door, I heard the phone. I went to the study and sat down at my desk before answering.

'Hi sweetheart, how are things?' It had been almost two weeks since I'd heard from Adam.

'Exhausting – I'm looking forward to coming over on Christmas Eve.'

'I just wondered if I might see you before then.'

'I'm frantically busy and Christmas Eve's just a few days away.'

He sounded disappointed and suggested a flying visit on Sunday. I gave in and said okay. He said he missed me and, in a more cheerful tone, added, 'Can't wait to see you.'

I picked up Peter's gift and shook it but nothing moved. It wasn't heavy so I thought it might be a piece of jewellery. My curiosity almost made me open it there and then, but I decided to wait, at least for a day or so. I took it upstairs and put it in my bedside table drawer.

Giles called again. I told him his order would be ready for delivery last thing tomorrow so we chatted about business.

The article by Sophie Williams in the Best of the West magazine had turned out better than expected and generated orders from three new customers. I now supplied eight shops on a regular basis which kept me busy almost seven days a week. It was the most I could cope with. I felt I'd reached my limit and the thought of my business growing any larger just didn't appeal to me, despite Giles' suggestion of supplying to supermarkets. I couldn't imagine my relishes being mass produced in a factory, but I knew this would be inevitable if demand kept increasing.

It then occurred to me how little time I was spending with Adam. We were seeing less and less of each other and only sending the odd text message now and again. Phone conversations had become a rarity. When we did speak, we always said how much we missed each other, but somehow the words were beginning to sound meaningless.

Green's was bustling with Christmas shoppers and Giles was darting around trying to do ten things at once. Jenny, his assistant, saw me struggling in the doorway and came to help me. I lowered the heavy cardboard box onto a sack truck which she wheeled through to the store room. She then followed me out to the car to collect another four boxes. Giles had made sure his stock would last well into the New Year.

As I waited near the entrance, I noticed a group of people standing around a pyramid-shaped display by the cheese counter. It was draped in red and green tinsel. They were carefully taking jars from the top, studying the contents, smiling then putting them in their baskets. Even from where I was standing, I recognised the distinct black and white labels and was pleased Giles had chosen to promote my relishes. I wandered over to take a closer look.

'I feel I should ask for your autograph.' I turned to see an attractive dark-haired man standing beside me. His hazel eyes gazed towards a copy of the Best of the West magazine which lay open on a nearby table. I blushed. I knew what he was thinking. I looked at the two jars in his basket and said, 'Hope you like it.' Before he could answer, I saw that Giles was free. 'Sorry, I must go and talk to the owner.' As I walked away, I heard him say, 'That's a shame.'

'Hello, having a busy day?' I said, grinning at Giles who looked drained.

'It's been manic but I've got some free time now. Let's go into my office.' He ushered me through the door behind the counter. 'Would you like a sherry? I've been meaning to try this. It's supposed to be excellent.' He picked up a bottle from his desk and held it at an angle so that I could read the label but the only Spanish word I recognised was Jerez. It looked good.

'I'd love one. Thanks.'

In amongst the chaos, he managed to find two tumblers. He poured a little sherry into each then handed one to me. 'Cheers.' He bumped his glass against mine and we both took a sip; its warm, mellow flavour lingered in my mouth.

'Here's to a successful festive season,' I said.

He smiled then asked what I was doing for Christmas. It was the first time anyone had been interested. I quickly said spending it with a friend, hoping to avoid any further questions, but he continued by asking if I was going away or staying at home.

'Actually Christmas isn't a happy time for me so I'd rather not talk about it, if you don't mind.'

'Oh, I'm sorry.' He looked at me curiously. 'Well, your relishes have been flying off the shelves, so well done for coming up with such a great product.'

He offered to top up my empty glass but I declined. He then produced a box of mince pies, but I shook my head. 'I'm afraid I can't stay long but thanks anyway – and thank you for being such a loyal customer. I really appreciate it.'

There was something very charming about Giles. Our relationship was a professional one and though it was tempting to delve into each other's private lives, we always kept our conversations above board. I wondered if he was married. There was no ring so I concluded he wasn't. He also liked to flirt with female customers. I admired him. He was young, attractive and a very shrewd businessman.

145

'So where do you think you'll be in five years' time?' he asked, looking straight at me.

'I really don't know,' I replied. It sounded vague and rather stupid. I wished I hadn't said it. 'I mean, I haven't made plans that far ahead. I'm happy with things as they are.'

He frowned and said a business needs constant development. There have to be goals. I understood what he was trying to tell me – if I didn't plan ahead, my business would fail. I knew that I constantly needed to come up with new ideas, but, apart from my Christmas gift box, I hadn't found the time to think of anything else.

'I'd better go. I'm sure you're needed in the shop. Thanks for the sherry.'

We walked to the door. I wished him a happy Christmas. He grinned and tactfully said he looked forward to seeing me again in the New Year.

As I drove home, I thought about Christmas. In a way, I was looking forward to it and being with Adam, but before then I had to cope with the anniversary of your death. It hung before me like a black cloud and I wondered if it would always be like that – sorrow before joy.

By the time I got back, it was dark. Clare had locked the outbuilding and gone. I went in to check everything was tidy. She had left it as expected, immaculately clean and everything in its place. She'd also left a Christmas card and a note saying, 'have a restful day tomorrow.' Unlikely, I thought, with Adam coming over first thing in the morning. I still hadn't found the courage to tell her about our relationship but what didn't concern her was probably not worth mentioning and might even spoil our friendship. I noticed she'd picked up the gift I'd left her. We weren't seeing each other again until the New Year and I was sorry I'd missed the chance to thank her and wish her a happy Christmas.

It had been an exhausting day and after cooking a meal, clearing away and finally sitting down to relax, it was almost time to go to bed. The thought of sleep seemed preferable to anything else, so I locked up, turned off the lights, and went upstairs.

Thoughts came and went so I tried to read for a while. It wasn't long before my mind began to wander again. It seemed impossible to concentrate so I closed the book and reached over to turn off the light. As my hand found the switch, I thought about Peter's gift in the drawer beneath. I'd been tempted to open it ever since he'd given it to me, but resisted thinking I should wait until Christmas day. Now my curiosity was getting the better of me. I took out the small box and held it up to the light. It had to be jewellery. I knew Peter cared for me, but somehow I couldn't imagine him buying me anything so personal. I tugged at the neatly-tied ribbon until it slid off, then tore away the paper until I was left with a plain white box. I gently lifted the lid. Inside, lay something oblong and slender wrapped in pink tissue paper. I carefully took off the paper and finally saw the object of my curiosity – a delicate, old glass scent bottle with a silver stopper, exquisitely decorated with small silver flowers cascading from the neck down each side. I took off the stopper. There was a faint, sweet odour that had faded to almost nothing. I wondered if it had belonged to his mother. It was beautiful. I put it on the bedside table and lay down mesmerised by the way the light made it sparkle. This was a gift to be treasured. It would always remind me of Peter.

Adam arrived early. I ran downstairs and just made it to the back door before he opened it and let himself in. His face was pink and his breath steaming from the cold. Before I could say anything, he handed me a carrier bag which contained some flowers and a box of chocolates. I thanked him with a kiss on the cheek and we walked into the kitchen. He hung his jacket on the back of a chair then came over and put his arms around me.

'It's been a while hasn't it?' His eyes expressed his thoughts and I sighed inwardly. I wasn't in the mood. In fact, I felt exhausted. 'Work's been so hectic I'm finding it difficult to sleep these days. To be honest, I feel drained,' I said assertively.

'Well, you'll soon get some rest. I've got everything organised for the big day. You won't have to do anything except eat, drink and be merry, I promise.' He then lifted up my chin with his forefinger and kissed me on the forehead. 'What would you like to do today? I thought maybe we could drive to the north coast somewhere. A change of scene would do us both good.'

'...Sounds perfect.' Getting away from the house and work was just what I needed.

'That's better. I was beginning to worry about you.'

'Sorry, there's just so much going on at the moment.' I was about to mention the anniversary of your death but stopped myself. It wasn't something I wanted to share with him. Tomorrow I would wake up and pretend it was just another day, until he had left for work. After that the day would be mine.

It was one of those crisp mornings where the frosted branches of trees and frozen clumps of earth glittered in the sun. I hoped it would be like this on Christmas day. We got into the car and set off towards the main road. Adam kept one hand on the steering wheel and one on my knee. I liked its warmth. From time to time we'd glance at each other. I felt too tired to talk and let my head fall back against the head rest. Soon I was fighting to stay awake and closed my eyes. The sun flickered for a while on my eyelids and then I must have fallen asleep.

It had only been a short nap but when I awoke, I felt refreshed.

'Sorry, I just couldn't keep my eyes open,' I said yawning and stretching my arms and legs out in front of me.

'That's fine. Just take it easy. I'm enjoying the drive.'

Adam was staring straight ahead. I turned on the radio and found a classical music station which seemed to complement our relaxed moods. The colour of the sky and passing fields seemed to be intensified by the clear light of the winter sun. Its beauty was mesmerising.

By the time we arrived at Watersmeet it was lunchtime so I suggested going on a bit further to the harbour where there were a few places to eat. Five minutes later we were pulling into a parking space near the quay. Adam turned off the engine.

'It's strange how the sea looks brown despite the sky being so blue,' I said looking at the dull expanse of water ahead of us and thinking how it usually reflects the colour of the sky.

'It's the Bristol Channel. It's always like this,' he replied. He didn't bother to explain why. 'Come on. Let's see if we can find somewhere to have lunch.'

We got out of the car. It was still bitterly cold, so I pulled up my scarf to cover my ears and put on some gloves. We put our arms round each other and walked briskly towards the nearest pub. The few small harbour-side shops were decked out with brightly-coloured baubles and fairy lights. There was a festive atmosphere with people buying last-minute gifts and, for the first time, I began to feel excited about Christmas. It would be different but Adam seemed determined to make it special and I felt grateful to him for that.

The Smugglers Inn was busy and we only managed to find a table because a family got up to leave. Adam went to the bar and came back with two glasses of mulled wine and a menu. We ordered roast beef which was served almost straight away and eaten at virtually the same speed to satisfy our hunger.

It was almost three when we left the pub so there was just enough time to stroll around the harbour before dusk. A few seagulls were scavenging along the sea wall. We leant on the cold, iron railings to watch them as they fought over some litter. The tide was out and the boats lay at precarious angles in the dark, sulphurous mud. Adam put his arm round my shoulder and pulled me towards him. 'I hope you're feeling better now,' he said. 'Work can take over your life if you let it, you know.'

The tone of his voice implied that he felt neglected. 'I'm sure it won't always be like this. It's just a very busy time of year. Besides, I enjoy what I do.'

He didn't answer.

'I know we haven't spent much time together lately, but we'll make up for it. I do miss you when you're not around,' I said.

He moved his arm away from my shoulder and took my hand. 'Let's go back.'

'Okay,' I said affectionately.

We slept soundly and I only woke because I heard Adam in the shower. It was seven-thirty on the first anniversary of your death. I rolled over. It felt wrong to be with someone else.

The bathroom door opened and Adam's naked body appeared in a cloud of steam. He sat on the bed and leant down to kiss me. 'Morning,' he whispered. 'You looked dead to the world. I'm sorry if I woke you.'

I rubbed my eyes. 'It's okay. I've got some things I need to do so I ought to get up. I'll make some breakfast.' I slipped out of bed, put on my dressing gown and, before he could answer, went out of the room.

On my way to the kitchen, I caught sight of the Christmas rose, its pot still wrapped in cellophane. I'd put it under the stairs away from direct sunlight. The drooping white flowers seemed to reflect my mood and I hung my head as if in acknowledgement.

I made a pot of tea and some toast and was just buttering it when Adam came bounding down the stairs. I looked at the clock; it was eight fifteen. He swept past me and picked up his jacket from the back of the chair.

'I'll have to skip breakfast, I'm afraid.'

'No, take it with you. I'll put it in some foil.' The toast was still warm as I wrapped it up. Adam drank some tea then took the silver parcel from me. 'See you tomorrow.' We kissed and he rushed out of the back door, slamming it behind him. I hadn't had the chance to reply.

I went back upstairs and lay down on the unmade bed. All the memories and pain I'd tried to suppress came flooding back and felt as raw as they did a year ago. The sounds and images, the sense of hopelessness and devastation were overwhelming and I tried to blot them out by burying my head in the pillow. For some reason, I couldn't cry.

It was a dull day. I'd gone back to sleep and when I woke, it was almost eleven. There was no rush to do anything so I got up and ran a bath. The room quickly filled with steam and as I sat on the edge, I tried to visualise you – and then I remembered – the time I saw you again – after the funeral.

I was lying in bed unable to sleep but I must have dozed off and only opened my eyes because I sensed someone was leaning over me. When I looked up, I saw your face. It was so real I asked you what you were doing here. There was a bright, shimmering light around you that lit up the room. It made you look radiant, like the sun. Your face was so close and you were smiling at me. You then lowered your head and I raised mine so that our lips could meet. I will always remember that kiss – its warmth flowed right through me, filling me with the purest form of love. Afterwards I slept so deeply, I didn't wake up until nine-thirty the following morning. I never told anyone about this, not even Ali. When I got up, I played your favourite Beatles' song 'All You Need Is Love' over and over again. It was so true. From that day on, I stopped sensing you around me and then I realised – you had come back to say goodbye.

I slid under the bath water until just my face and knees broke the surface. In a feeble voice, I started to sing 'All you need is love…la-la-la-la-la…..All you need is love, love….All you need is love…'

The churchyard was only a ten-minute stroll from the cottage. I walked quickly hoping I wouldn't be seen. It still

151

hurt too much to talk about you.

The small church sat at the entrance to a large estate which had once employed the entire community. It was falling into disrepair, but I remembered how you had been captivated by its beauty the moment we walked through the gate. We'd wandered between the graves reading the headstones and then you said, 'this is where I want to be buried.' You said it with such conviction I wondered if you knew your life would be cut short.

It had been a few months since I'd visited your grave and as I approached the plaque that lay near the path, my heart sank. The small, bleak stone and the words on its surface seemed so insignificant. Your happy, vibrant life had been extinguished like a candle flame and this was all that was left. 'John Chester, 1946 – 2008. Much loved and sorely missed.' There wasn't room for anything else.

I gently brushed away the leaves then opened the carrier bag containing the Christmas rose and a trowel. The earth was hard, but the trowel's sharp blade cut through the surface with relative ease. I dug almost frantically, spurred on by a deep sense of guilt. I'd neglected you – left nature to almost obscure you. I should have visited you more often. I should have surrounded your grave with flowers, not waited so long. Hot tears dripped onto the soil. I fumbled in my pocket for a tissue then hurriedly put the plant in the ground. I pushed the earth back and pressed it down against the stem, then used the carrier bag to collect some water from a trough near the gate. I poured some around the base and watched as the flower heads lifted slightly. Now there would always be beauty around you. I put the empty pot and trowel back in the bag and walked towards the gate. As I left the churchyard, I looked back and saw a solitary robin pecking at the freshly dug earth. I closed the gate and it flew up to a nearby tree. A few moments later, it began to sing.

Chapter 16

It was Christmas Eve and I was in the middle of breakfast when Adam called – he wanted me to come over as soon as I could. His voice was full of excitement. I tried to reciprocate but it was hard to convey something I didn't really feel.

'What's up? You don't sound very keen.'

'I'm fine. I'll be over in an hour or so. I've just got some last minute things to do.'

'Okay – whenever you're ready.' He put the phone down without saying goodbye. I sensed he was annoyed but I was sure things would be okay once we were together.

Being alone in the home where I'd shared so many Christmases with you felt strange and empty. A few days ago it had been a hive of activity but now everything had been replaced by an eerie silence. I went upstairs to fetch my holdall and the bag of presents I'd left on the bed. The room was tidy apart from a few clothes draped over the bedroom chair. Before I closed the door, I remembered Peter's scent bottle. I couldn't resist having another look at it so I went over to the bedside table and took the box out of the drawer. As I lifted the lid, I saw a small fleck of white lying on top of the pink tissue paper. I tried to brush it away but it stuck to my finger. I looked at it more closely and noticed from its shape and texture that it was another feather – the smallest I'd found so far.

I'd been in bed when I first opened the box so a feather from my bedding could have easily fallen inside. It was the first time I'd come up with a plausible explanation so I brushed it away and pulled back the tissue paper to expose the bottle. It was so delicate and beautiful. I couldn't wait to ask Peter about it.

The feather had fallen onto the floor and stood out against the beige carpet. Its bright white fronds spread out like a small fan. I couldn't take my eyes off it so I bent

153

down to pick it up and, without thinking, put it back in the box and closed the lid.

As I drove away from the cottage, all the previous day's sadness drifted away and I looked forward to being with Adam again.

I tried not to think beyond Christmas, but it was difficult. Just dealing with all the emails sitting in my inbox would be bad enough but then I thought of all the jobs I'd put on hold. A wave of anxiety rose up inside me but I couldn't let this dominate my thoughts – not for the next few days at least.

I managed to park close to the house. The gate was open and just as I was about to walk up the path Adam appeared. He took my bags from me and I followed him into the hallway then shut the front door. After putting them down, we kissed and wished each other happy Christmas.

'This looks really festive,' I said impressed by the bright red and green swag hanging underneath the bannister on the stairs.

'You haven't seen anything yet – come into the sitting room.'

Although the room was small, he'd managed to squeeze a six-foot Christmas tree into the alcove between the window and the fireplace. It was beautifully decorated with large gold and silver baubles that sparkled each time they were illuminated by the flashing fairy lights. A row of white scented candles glowed on the coffee table and the whole room was filled with the heady smell of fresh pine, cinnamon and wood smoke. It was perfect. I fetched the bag of presents from the hall and Adam watched me put them under the tree. Afterwards I stood up and turned to hug him but he'd gone into the kitchen.

'Let's have a drink before lunch,' he said, opening the fridge and taking out a bottle of Cava.

'I think you've done a fantastic job. The tree looks amazing.' I went over to put my arms round him but he moved away. 'Are you okay?' I asked sensing he wasn't.

'I'm fine and I'll feel even better after a drink.' He took a couple of glasses out of the cupboard. After prizing out the cork, he carefully filled them with the fizzing wine and handed me a glass. 'Here's to us and absent...' He paused.

'...family and friends?' I finished the sentence for him. 'It's okay. Don't worry about it.' It was a crass mistake but I tried to smile as if it hadn't affected me. 'Are you seeing your daughters over Christmas?'

'Yes, they're coming over the day after Boxing Day. I'm taking them out for lunch.'

'Great. I'll make sure I leave early. I intend to work that day anyway.' Our conversation was strained and I felt awkward. Something was bugging Adam and I needed to find out what. 'I've been really looking forward to this, believe me.'

'Have you?' He sounded surprised. 'I suppose getting away makes things a little easier but I do appreciate it's not a good time for you. I'm sorry for putting my foot in it earlier.'

'Adam – please relax. I want us to enjoy Christmas. You don't have to treat me with kid gloves.' I put my glass on the table then walked over and stood behind him, slipping my arms round his waist and snuggling up against him.

He put his glass down and turned round. We held each other's gaze then he kissed me gently on the forehead as if to apologise. Afterwards we took our drinks into the lounge. He seemed to be his old self again. I sat on the sofa and watched him stoke up the fire. The room was cosy and the wine was going to my head. I picked up the book I'd brought with me and curled up waiting for him to come and sit next to me, but he stood up and walked back towards the door. 'I'll see to lunch.' His voice sounded flat. There was definitely something wrong but I wasn't in the mood to find out. It was Christmas and the last thing I wanted was a row.

The smell of cooked meat was making me hungry. I

looked at my watch. I'd been reading for half an hour. There was hardly a sound coming from the kitchen so I put down my book and went to see if Adam needed any help. The table was laid, the meat was resting on a plate and vegetables were simmering on the stove but he wasn't anywhere to be seen. I looked through the window thinking he might have gone outside but there was no sign of him. I went to the bottom of the stairs and called out, 'Adam. Are you up there?' There was no reply. Then, the front door opened and he walked in. 'Sorry, I should have told you I was going out.'

I stared at him. 'Where have you been?'

'I needed some fresh air, that's all.'

'What's the matter?'

'Nothing, I'm fine.' He took off his jacket and hung it on one of the coat hooks behind the door.

'I'll finish preparing lunch if you like,' I said. 'You go and relax in the sitting room.' He looked anxious and it was making me feel uneasy.

'No, everything's ready. I've just got to dish it up.'

I followed him into the kitchen and leant against one of the units. 'Did you go down to the sea front?'

He took the vegetables over to the sink to strain them. 'No; just along the lane,' he said without looking at me.

'Adam, I know there's something wrong. What is it?' The prospect of spending Christmas with him in such low spirits was worrying. We had to clear the air.

'I've had some news which I don't want to talk about right now. I'm sorry. I'll be okay. Just give me a bit of space. We'll discuss it later.'

I was stunned. What news? The words cut into me. It had to be bad to make him so unhappy. I'd never seen him like this before.

'Please let's try and enjoy the next couple of days.' I went to the fridge and took out the bottle of Cava. 'Would you like a refill?' I topped up my glass. Adam turned and nodded. He then put the roast pork and vegetables on the table and we sat down.

156

'This looks delicious,' I said, trying to cheer him up.

His blue eyes slowly began to sparkle again as he raised his glass. 'You're right Susie, let's make this Christmas special.'

A wave of relief drifted over me. There was a right time and place for everything and now was not the right time to discuss his problems, whatever they might be.

It was Christmas morning. Adam had already gone downstairs. I turned over, disappointed to be alone. We had gone to bed early the night before but there had been hardly any affection between us. We'd kissed and then gone straight to sleep. I looked at the space where he'd slept and thought of the times after your funeral I'd longed to see you lying next to me. This time, as I stared at the crumpled pillow, I felt hurt and wondered why he couldn't have waited for me to wake up before going downstairs. The more I thought about it, the more I became upset so I got up and walked over to the window. The sea was calm and the sun's rays were trying to break through the white mist that hung above it. There was something magical about the light, and I couldn't help thinking of you. If heaven exists, then I was sure you were there. I pressed my hand on the cold pane of glass knowing that you were somewhere on the other side.

The sound of Adam's footsteps on the stairs made me rush back to bed. I quickly slid under the duvet and lay on my side pretending to be asleep.

'Hey sleepy head, wake up. I've brought you some coffee.'

I turned over and opened my eyes. 'Oh – thanks.' I sat up and took the mug from him then put it on the bedside table. He bent down and kissed the top of my head then took off his dressing gown and got back into bed. 'Happy Christmas sweetheart – come here.' He pulled me towards him and we started to make love. Despite my earlier feelings, I allowed him to savour every part of me. Afterwards we lay close to each other and he stroked my

157

hair. I tried not to think of anything else but suddenly I pictured you. I let the thought linger. I closed my eyes and imagined your face. I knew it was wrong, but I wanted him so much to be you. Then I felt him get out of bed. I continued to lie still, pretending to doze. I heard clattering from the kitchen and left him to get on with the task of preparing Christmas lunch – his words 'you won't have to do anything ...' easing my guilty conscience. When he eventually came back upstairs, I'd showered and was getting dressed. As he walked past me to the bathroom, he said, 'The turkey's in the oven. All we have to do now is open the champagne.'

'Sounds perfect,' I said as I struggled into my favourite red dress. He stopped to help me with the zip and kissed the back of my neck. 'You look lovely.' He was looking at my reflection in the full length mirror.

'Thanks sweetheart,' I said looking back at him. He then went into the bathroom and closed the door. After putting on some make up and brushing my hair, I went downstairs. Adam's efforts to make the day special were everywhere – a crackling log fire, twinkling lights on the Christmas tree and carols playing in the background. I was touched, but then I remembered the news he hadn't wanted to share with me. Perhaps it was a family problem and none of my business. I hoped today wouldn't be the day I found out.

I put another log on the fire and was just about to go into the kitchen when Adam appeared looking relaxed and handsome. His deep blue eyes enhanced by the colour of his pale blue shirt.

'Time to open the champers,' he said grinning. 'Sit down and make yourself comfortable, I'll be back in a second.'

I sank onto the sofa, bemused by his attentiveness. He soon returned with two glasses of buck's fizz. After handing me a glass, he sat down next to me. 'Happy Christmas and thanks for looking after me so well,' I said and leant over to kiss him on the cheek.

'Happy Christmas to you too sweetheart – I think you deserve to be spoilt – today of all days,' he replied.

Breakfast was another buck's fizz plus a toasted muffin topped with smoked salmon and scrambled egg which we ate slowly while putting the world to rights. It seemed so absurd to be discussing politics on Christmas morning, we dissolved into laughter. Afterwards, I cleared everything away before Adam could stop me. What followed seemed rather hazy but we decided to give each other one present to open so we went back to the sitting room. Adam sat on the sofa and I knelt down by the Christmas tree to look for the gift I knew he would like the most. He'd pointed out a watch to me a few weeks ago which he'd wanted to buy so I was relieved to see he was still wearing his old one.

I eventually uncovered the small box and handed it to him. His gift to me was much larger wrapped in red paper and tied with a gold ribbon. I read the label which said simply, 'To my darling Susie with love from Adam' followed by three kisses. I knew from its softness that it had to be some sort of clothing.

Adam smiled knowingly at me and said, 'I wonder what this could be?' He glanced at his watch.

'Something very useful,' I replied. 'I know you're going to like it.'

'Hmm – we'll see.' He pulled off the wrapping paper and uncovered the white box which just had the manufacturer's name printed in the centre. His eyes lit up as he opened it. 'Thank you so much sweetheart. It's a good job I didn't get round to buying this.' He immediately took off his old watch and put on the new one, holding his arm up to admire it then he thanked me with a warm and forceful kiss on the lips. 'It's perfect.'

I carefully removed the wrapping paper from my present to reveal a soft, grey jumper. I held it up against myself and immediately knew it would fit, despite its large size. It was also long enough to wear with leggings. 'Thank you. It's lovely.' I hugged and kissed him.

The rest of the day was spent in a comfortable state of

wooziness. After lunch we lay on the sofa to watch a DVD but fell asleep and only woke because the fire had gone out and the room felt cold. By nine-thirty we were ready for bed.

We got up late on Boxing Day and after a quick breakfast went out for a long walk. My head was still spinning from the day before so I welcomed the thought of some fresh air. There was a slight mist that looked as though it would clear once the sun came out. Neither of us felt particularly talkative so we left the house and walked towards the steep path that led down to the beach. It was muddy so Adam went ahead and I followed trying not to slip over. The distance between us widened and I was about to call out to him to wait when his phone rang. He stopped to answer it. He looked up at me then turned away lowering his voice. As I caught up with him, I heard him quickly end the call with 'speak to you later, bye.'

'Who was that?' I asked.

'Oh, just Becky checking what time to come over tomorrow,' he replied looking away. He was frowning and seemed concerned about something. 'I told her we were out walking.' He bit his lower lip and slipped his phone back into his pocket.

'Did she say something to upset you?'

'No – not at all – everything's fine.'

I sensed that it wasn't but let the matter go. It was probably something to do with the news he'd had which I assumed he still didn't want to talk about.

When we reached the beach, he took my hand. The sea breeze was damp and bitterly cold. It penetrated my clothes and made me shiver, but I inhaled the icy air into my lungs hoping it would clear my head.

The shingle crunched under our shoes then fell away so that our feet sank with each step. Walking was difficult and we were making slow progress. After a while, he suggested we go and sit by the water's edge. Something in his voice made me feel tense. The beach shelved down to a flat ridge and then again down to the sea. Adam let go of my hand and half-walked, half-slid to the edge of the ridge then sat down with his back to me. I followed and almost fell down next to him waiting for him to put his arm round me but he didn't. Instead he picked up a pebble and flung it towards the sea. I watched it plop into the spume of a receding wave.

'We need to talk, Susie,' he said.

I couldn't answer and braced myself for something bad. He turned to look at me but I couldn't look at him. I didn't want to see the expression on his face.

'After we'd met at Beth and Steve's party, I knew I'd fallen for you in a big way. The chemistry between us was incredible, wasn't it?' He waited for me to respond but I didn't. My heart was thumping and hurting at the same time and I began to feel sick.

'Look at me Susie, please. I do love you.'

His eyes were probing mine and I could see they were filling with tears. 'No you don't.' I wanted to explain what real love was like – the love I'd felt for you – a deep and everlasting love that was ingrained in each other's souls – but I just stared at him, waiting to hear what else he had to say. My nausea was slowly turning to anger.

'I didn't want to tell you this until the time felt right, but then I thought there may never be a right time, so I'm going to tell now.' He took my hand and squeezed it hard. 'I'm going back to Jane, my ex-wife. We want to try again. Make it work.'

Each word exploded in my head – and all I could say was, 'Oh really?'

The icy wind made me feel numb. I pulled my hand away from his and stood up. 'I'd better go then.' Somehow I managed not to cry as I tried to run back up the bank of shingle. My determination to get away from him made me resort to all fours and scramble as fast as I could back up to the flat part of the beach.

'Susie, wait... wait...'

I heard him coming after me. 'Go to hell Adam

161

Walker.' Then the tears came, hot and blinding. I headed towards the path, my legs aching from the effort of running on shingle and into the wind. I knew Adam could hear my uncontrollable sobs. He called out again. His voice was louder this time. '...Susie – for God's sake.' He was closing in on me but I managed to reach the path and then I stopped to catch my breath. My sobbing was making me cough until I felt I might choke – and then I retched and let the contents of my stomach splatter and splash onto the pebbles, its acrid smell rising up and drifting away on the wind.

'Jesus, I'm so sorry.' Adam was rubbing my back. I could see traces of vomit in my hair and I could feel it around my mouth. I searched in my jacket pockets for a tissue and found one that had already been used. I tried to clean myself up but my hands were trembling. 'Just go away and leave me alone. I'll see you back at the house when I'm feeling better.'

'I didn't want it to end like this.' He walked up the path with his head down.

I watched him until he'd reached the top and disappeared from view. I was in no hurry to go back, even though I was chilled to the bone. There was nothing more to say to each other. I would just go in, gather up my things and leave.

The numbness I'd felt earlier returned and I walked aimlessly trying to make sense of what had just happened. I was alone again but this time it was different. The pain was mixed with anger, not sadness. I felt confused and humiliated. I thought I'd got my life back together but today it had been shattered into a thousand pieces. I was back to square one. I should have listened to Ali and Peter. They saw Adam wasn't right for me but I was lonely and the attraction between us too strong to resist. It was obvious now that our relationship had been based merely on lust. There had only ever been one love in my life – you. God, what a stupid idiot I've been.

The sun had come out and I looked up hoping its

162

silvery rays could somehow soothe me. I'd been walking for a long time and needed to get back. I needed to get away from Adam. I was deeply wounded but I knew I'd get over it. I still had my business and I had friends. Soon I would see Peter again – a beacon of light in all of this gloom.

I opened the gate to the cottage and hesitated. The front door was firmly closed. I would have to knock to be let in. Then I saw Adam looking through the sitting room window. Within a few seconds the front door opened and I stepped into the hall. He was standing by the door and our bodies touched as I walked past. I couldn't bring myself to look at him.

'Susie, you're freezing. Please go and sit by the fire. I'll get you a brandy.'

I went into the sitting room, still wearing my jacket which I noticed had a few splashes of vomit on the sleeve. I took it off and put it on the arm of the chair. My hands were blue with cold. The room still looked festive but the lights on the tree had been switched off as if to mark the end of Christmas – and us. I couldn't speak. All I could do was stare blankly at the fire. Adam put a small glass down on the side table next to me then sat on the sofa.

'Please don't say you're sorry,' I said. 'What hurts more than anything else is that you've been seeing Jane behind my back – how could you be so deceitful?'

'I didn't know what to do – how or when to tell you.' His voice wavered. 'I wanted to share Christmas with you.'

I glared at him then sipped my drink. There was no point to this conversation, no point at all. 'I'd better go.' The ache in my stomach returned. 'I'll just get my things.'

Adam didn't reply. I went upstairs and stuffed everything into my holdall, leaving the jumper he'd bought me lying on the bed. He could take it back to the shop. I didn't need a constant reminder of him. The word 'bastard' formed in my mind and then I said it: 'You bloody bastard.' Then I felt his hand on my arm, gripping

163

it tightly. He pulled me up but I pushed at his chest and struggled until I was free of him. The effort made me fall back onto the bed. I got up and grabbed my bag. 'Get out of my way. I want to go home.'

'Susie, please I need to explain. I still care for you very much.... But...'

I didn't want to hear any more. I pushed past him and ran down the stairs then out of the house. When I reached my car, I turned to see him standing at the gate with his face buried in his hands. In spite of all the good times we'd shared, I knew that was how I'd always remember him. As I drove away, I glanced in my rear view mirror. He'd gone back into the house.

Chapter 17

I could have easily wallowed in self-pity but there was too much to do. My business was now my priority. I'd suffered a blow but it wasn't the end of the world. Deep down, I'd always felt that Adam might leave me for someone else so there was no point thinking about what might have been. He'd gone back to Jane because she'd offered him something I couldn't – a future. My biggest regret was telling him I loved him. It had been a lie. Another chapter of my life had come and gone. When I thought about everything we'd done together, it made me feel sad – but not devastated. It had been good while it lasted. Images of him came and went but the one that remained was the one that had left a lasting impression – a man who looked lost and confused with his head in his hands.

There were fewer emails in my inbox than anticipated which gave me time to think about the direction of my business. The asparagus relish was undoubtedly my best seller and I began to consider dropping the others. Although sales had been steady, they hadn't taken off in the same way. Peter would be ready to plant up the vegetable garden in the spring and it now seemed sensible to devote it to asparagus, even though the beds would take a few years to become established.

I wondered what sort of Christmas he'd had. It would be difficult to avoid telling him about mine. He'd been right about Adam all along which intrigued me, particularly as they'd never met – but then I remembered the way he'd watched us from a distance at Beth's fair and how he'd disappeared when I caught his eye. There was also his gift. Maybe he was fonder of me than I realised. It had been just under a year since we first met but I still didn't know him – and yet there was a strong bond between us. It reminded me of the familiarity couples have

165

when they've been together a long time but without the physical intimacy. We'd become good friends because we trusted each other. He was also dependable and selfless, always putting my interests first. It was rare to meet a man with his qualities and I wished I felt physically attracted to him, but I didn't. There was no chemistry and probably never would be.

In a way, my life had gone full circle. I was alone again but the fear and emptiness I'd felt a year ago had been replaced by a new sense of purpose. Survival wasn't something I'd really understood until now. I'd come through the worst experience of my life and felt stronger as a result. The human spirit is remarkable. It can endure so much.

The sound of a car pulling up outside made me go to the window. Whoever it was had parked in the layby next to the cottage. I opened the front door and stepped outside. Two car doors slammed and I heard voices.

'Hey – long time, no see!' Ali came towards me with her arms outstretched. We hugged each other for a few seconds and then she let go so that David could say hello and kiss me on the cheek.

'Why didn't you tell me you were coming?' I said – trying to smile with tears in my eyes.

'We wanted to surprise you both.' Ali took off her coat and put it on the back of the sofa. She looked around the sitting room. 'Is Adam here?'

'No. Why don't you sit down and I'll make some tea, unless you'd like something stronger?' The room felt cold and I apologised. 'I'll just go and put the central heating on. I wasn't expecting any visitors.' I ran upstairs. On my way back down, I saw David kneeling by the wood burner trying to make a fire. 'Oh, you don't have to do that,' I said with embarrassment.

He smiled. 'It's okay. I'm just trying to prove something you said some time ago about men who make good fires.'

We all laughed.

'So – where's Adam?' Ali asked.

'I might as well tell you. He's not here because we're not seeing each other anymore.'

'What?' She looked astounded. 'Why?'

'He's decided to go back to his wife, Jane.'

Before I could say anything else, she was putting her arms around me. 'God, I'm so sorry. What a bloody awful Christmas you must have had.' But her face expressed what she'd really wanted to say which was 'I told you so.'

'I'm okay – honestly,' I said, moving away from her. David got up and went into the kitchen. Moments later I heard cupboards being opened and the kettle being filled with water.

'How was your Christmas?' I asked.

'Great. We had David's mother to stay. She went home yesterday.' Ali looked towards the kitchen. 'I don't know what to say about Adam except that I never really liked him from the start. He was too smooth – too good-looking.'

'I know but I just fell for him. I couldn't help it, but I knew it wouldn't last. He wasn't John.'

'No, he wasn't.'

'Let's change the subject. What's done is done. I hate post mortems.'

Ali's eyes widened. 'Okay, sorry, I thought you might have wanted to talk about it.'

David came back carrying three mugs of tea which he put on the coffee table. My abruptness towards Ali had surprised both of us. David sat next to her and I sat down on the rug by the fire. 'Thanks.' I said, picking up one of the mugs. 'Well, it's back to work tomorrow. I'm looking forward to getting stuck in again. My asparagus relish is selling really well.'

'We tried it and thought it was superb. There's a distinct flavour that makes your mouth water. Maybe that's how it affects your libido? It excites the mouth first and then the rest of you,' David said, grinning. He

167

squeezed Ali's right knee as if to acknowledge its effect. They seemed so relaxed and happy together, it made me envious. It also hurt to think how much Ali had changed. Her constant fawning over David began to annoy me. 'I hope you're feeling a bit warmer now,' I said staring into the fire. There was no reply. I looked at them but they were too absorbed in each other to answer. David had whispered something that had made Ali blush. I got up and went into the kitchen. 'Would you like some more tea?' I yelled loudly.

'No thanks. We're fine,' Ali shouted back.

I stood in the doorway. 'Actually I've just remembered something I need to do before tomorrow – hope you don't mind.' I tried to hide the irritation in my voice.

'Oh, does that mean you want us to go then?' Ali said sharply.

'Maybe we can get together in a week or so for dinner. I wasn't expecting you to drop in so you've taken me by surprise. I also don't feel like being sociable at the moment. I suppose you've caught me at a bad time.'

'Never mind, we'll catch up again soon.' She tried to hide her disappointment by rummaging in her handbag. 'I nearly forgot – your Christmas present. Sorry it's late.' She handed me a small, neatly-wrapped parcel. 'Thanks for yours. It arrived Christmas Eve.'

I put the gift on the coffee table. 'Thank you. I'll open it later if that's okay.'

David stood up and helped Ali on with her coat. 'We'll be in touch. We should have called first,' he said apologetically.

'It's been good to see you.' I showed them out and shut the door, almost sighing with relief. Ali had changed. I had too, and no longer saw her as the supportive person I'd always been able to count on. Her loyalty was towards David now. I also became aware of the anger I felt towards her. It was a new emotion that was starting to gnaw away inside me.

I went up to the barn to take stock of what I needed to buy. There were still enough jars of relish left to make up any orders that might come in. Everything looked neat and organised and I thought about Clare – which in turn made me think about Adam and how happy he must be. Resentment churned away inside me as I pictured him back with his family. He probably hadn't given me another thought. Then, in a flash of anger, I reached for an empty jar and flung it onto the stone floor, oblivious to the shards of glass flying in all directions. 'God – what have I done to deserve this?' I screamed. My heart was pounding with fury. I was too angry to cry. As I opened the store cupboard to get the vacuum cleaner, someone walked into the barn. At first, I thought it was Adam and then I looked again. It was Peter. He stood still by the entrance, framed by the light. He'd caught me off guard and for a moment I thought I'd imagined him, the light around him was so bright.

He looked at the broken glass on the floor and then at me. 'I was just passing and saw your car outside so I thought I'd call in to see how you were.'

I didn't know whether to laugh or cry as I tried to pull the vacuum cleaner out of the cupboard. 'I've had a bit of an accident. It won't take long to clear up. The jar just slid through my fingers.'

'Someone's upset you, haven't they?' He was staring intently at me and I began to feel self-conscious. He then came towards me and I thought he was going to put his arms around me, but he stopped about two feet away and put his hand on my arm. 'You can tell me, Susie.' The gentleness of his touch and caring words were soothing and I began to relax. When he took his hand away, I felt instilled with an overwhelming sense of peace. It was the same sensation I'd experienced some months ago when he'd tried to console me under the ash tree. He'd put his hand on my arm in almost exactly the same spot and the effect had left me feeling almost euphoric. 'Look, I don't want to burden you with my problems.'

'It's Adam, isn't it? He's upset you, I know he has.'

'No – please, I don't want to talk about him. Not now.' It seemed as though my answer confirmed his suspicions. He looked at me and then he looked down. 'I knew this would happen.'

'How could you possibly know?' I asked. 'You've never met the man.'

'Call it foresight – a sixth sense. I just know things.' His eyes were fixed on mine. We stood motionless just staring at each other and then he said, 'Everything happens for a reason. It's a bit like climbing a mountain. We have to make choices about how we reach the summit. Sometimes they're wrong and we pay the price, but we learn from our mistakes and pick ourselves up and carry on because we know that the view from the top will be well worth the effort.'

He seemed to be looking into me not at me. His eyes were penetrating and I wondered what he could see. It made me feel uneasy. 'I suppose some of us don't always make it to the summit. Life defeats us. We give up,' I said warily.

'That's true, but those people aren't rewarded.' His eyes suddenly narrowed and I felt as though he was preaching to me.

'How do you know?' I felt I was venturing into unknown territory, but instead of answering me, he lifted his right hand and placed it gently on the top of my head. At first I wanted to laugh but as the heat flowed over my scalp, I felt uneasy and ducked away from him.

'I'm only trying to help you, Susie.'

'I'm not sure what you're trying to prove.'

For the first time since we'd met each other, I wanted him to leave.

He looked embarrassed and I felt guilty. 'I'm sorry, it's just that I've had a difficult few days.'

'It's okay. I just wanted to make you feel better. If you want to talk about it, I'm happy to listen but I think you'd rather just put it out of your mind and I could help you do that. I didn't mean to frighten you. I have the power to heal because I believe in God, that's all. It's a gift.'

I couldn't answer. It was the first time Peter had been so assertive and I now realised why he seemed different to other men. He walked around the work station to the other side and sat on a stool. He then clasped his hands together and let them rest on the work top. For a moment I thought he was praying.

We didn't speak for a while and then I said quietly, 'By the way, thank you for your present. Where on earth did you find it? It's beautiful.'

'Oh, that, yes,' he said, as if his mind was on something else. 'It was buried underneath a huge piece of flint in one of the flower beds. I had to dig down quite a way to get it out. Then I spotted something shiny that looked like silver. I dug the rest of the earth away with my hands. The bottle was in a terrible state so I took it home and cleaned it up so that I could give it to you. I knew you'd like it.'

I was somehow disappointed that it had come from the garden. It was mine anyway. 'I shall always treasure it Peter. It's beautiful.'

His eyes softened and he looked cheerful again. 'Thanks for the relishes. They went down very well on Christmas Day.'

'Did your father like them?'

'Yes, yes he did,' he said quietly. I waited for him to say something else, but he didn't. Instead he stood up and pushed the stool back under the work top. 'Well, I think I'd better get going. Everything's going to be okay Susie, you'll see.' His words were comforting and he patted my arm again before walking towards the door. As he opened it, he turned to smile at me, and then he was gone.

I switched on the vacuum cleaner and swept up the fragments of glass. So my future was all mapped out and I had nothing to worry about. How many times had I heard that before? But there was definitely something intriguing about Peter. He was the most extraordinary man I'd ever met.

171

Clare's enthusiasm to get back to work was refreshing. She burst into the barn like a ray of sunshine, looking stylish even in a pair of old, faded jeans and chunky blue sweater. I braced myself for the inevitable question about Christmas and when it came I forced a smile and said it had been fun. She said hers had been good too but then she made a surprising confession – that she actually hated the whole festive thing and what it now stood for. We both went through a long list of dislikes ranging from 'too commercial' to 'same old films' and 'eating and drinking far too much.' I was heartened to know that someone else shared my sentiments. It seemed that even our feelings towards Adam Walker were now mutual. The thought amused me. We chatted for a while longer and then I left her to make up some orders. I needed to finish some paperwork in the study.

I'd been thinking about launching a website and decided that Giles would probably be the best person to talk to about it so I phoned him. When he finally answered, I quickly wished him a Happy New Year then moved the conversation on to avoid the tedium of talking about Christmas all over again. He told me that my relishes had been one of his top sellers which gave me a much needed boost. He also said he would help me build a website with the aim of directing people to local stockists so that he would benefit too.

The New Year was getting off to a good start and I hung on to Peter's words that 'everything was going to be all right.' From now on, I would always believe him.

Orders began to come in again and the production of my most popular relish got back into full swing. I'd missed the smell of freshly chopped onions and the delicate fruity aroma of wine, asparagus and oranges simmering on the stove. Clare had got her food preparation down to a fine art and I loved watching her wash and roughly chop the ingredients then put them into one of several pans and after adding the correct amount of sugar, vinegar and white wine, stand and patiently stir the mixture until it came to the boil. Then she'd leave it to simmer until it was ready to take off the stove, cool and put into jars. Every move was smooth and militarily precise.

Giles was due to come over at the end of the week so I had time to go out and see customers. I wanted to do some market research and find out what shoppers thought of my relishes. It would be good to put some quotes online.

The first shop on my list was Ellie's Deli – a small business that had been set up by a couple who'd retired to the West Country. They also ran a smallholding where they grew their own produce and kept a few pigs and sheep. Ellie ran the delicatessen and her husband Nick took care of everything else. They'd moved from London so adapting to a slower pace of life had not been easy, but they were getting the hang of it.

As I pulled into the car park, a brood of chickens scattered in all directions and a dog started barking. Nick was up a ladder pruning a plum tree.

'Well, if it's not the raunchy relish lady,' he said waving a saw at me.

'Hi, how are you?' I said after slamming the car door.

'Not so bad. Glad Christmas is over though. All that feasting gets wearing after a while.'

'I couldn't agree more,' I said and walked towards the shop that looked as though it had once been a large wooden garage. One by one the chickens returned to scratch in the gravel – their gentle clucking and squawking a sign of their contentment.

Ellie was topping up the cheese counter with a few lumps of stilton when I walked in. 'Hello Susie – how are you?'

'I'm fine thanks. I thought I'd just pop in to wish you a Happy New Year and find out how my relishes are selling.' I looked around but couldn't see them.

'We sold out over Christmas and I meant to order more but just never found the time. We tried some too and loved it. Well, we thought, you know, being an aphrodisiac it

173

might spice up our Christmas.'

'And did it?' I asked curiously.

'I suppose, having drunk far too much, the effect was somewhat diluted, but we enjoyed it anyway.'

'I'm pleased to hear it,' I said, not certain what she was referring to. 'By the way, I'm setting up a website and wanted to add some testimonials, so could I add a comment from you?'

Ellie raised her eyebrows.

'No, seriously, it's publicity for your business too. I'll be listing all my stockists.'

'Okay, I think I'll have to ask Nick to come up with something, he's the PR man.'

'Great. Email it to me when you're ready.' I looked around the shop at the handwritten labels on piles of recycled wooden crates that were stacked to look like shelving. The locally-sourced range of foods was impressive and the words 'organic', 'no additives' and 'natural' were highlighted in yellow to stand out. One corner was devoted to a range of highly-perfumed, handmade soaps and natural cosmetics and another to locally-made pottery and willow baskets. It was an eclectic mix and a welcoming feast for the eyes.

Ellie's age was difficult to determine. I imagined her to be younger than she looked. Her long, grey hair pinned up with just a few strands left hanging around her pale, thin face aged her but her skin was smooth. She reminded me of a small bird as she darted from the cheese counter to the store room and back again laden with boxes.

'I can take another order from you while I'm here if you like?' I said, thinking it would save her time.

'No, don't worry. I need to work out what I want, but I promise I'll be in touch later this week. I'll get Nick to write a testimonial. He'll probably come up with something like 'fruity and exciting', knowing him.'

I laughed and wished her well then walked towards the door. The chickens had gathered at the back of my car but Nick shooed them away for me.

'I love them but they can be a pain in the arse sometimes,' he said grinning. '… never dreamt I'd end up eating them though – it's like devouring a member of the family.' He brushed the back of his hand over his greying hair. Unlike Ellie's, it was thick and wavy.

'I know what you mean.' The thought was repulsive. 'Well, I'd better get going – things to do, people to see.' I got in my car and waved through the window. Nick climbed back up his ladder.

By four o'clock I felt tired. I'd covered almost a hundred miles but every customer had been positive about my relishes and I drove home on a high. I tuned in the radio to my favourite music station and sang along at the top of my voice, even if I didn't know the words. For the first time in weeks, I felt good. It wasn't until I reached Hinton that my mood changed. The familiar pub sign for The Fox slowly emerged and as I drove past, I couldn't stop thoughts of Adam creeping into my head. It had been our favourite pub. I could still picture him reaching for my hand across the table then lifting it up to kiss it. I could feel his warm lips on my skin – each image more powerful than the last. I turned off the radio. The music got on my nerves. This wasn't how I'd wanted the day to end.

It was late when I got home and Clare had already gone. I knew she would have left everything shipshape before locking up the barn so I didn't bother to go and check. I gathered up some letters lying on the door mat and put them on the coffee table. I needed a drink so poured myself a large glass of cold white wine then sat down on the sofa to relax. A sudden bleep from my phone made me pick it up and scan through my messages. One was from Beth who wanted to see me about another charity event and have lunch with her on Saturday. It wasn't difficult to read between the lines. She'd probably heard that Adam and I were no longer together and thought I needed to talk about it, which I didn't, but I couldn't think of an excuse, and anyway I hadn't seen her for a while so I texted her back and accepted her invitation.

I hadn't eaten since lunch time so I searched in the freezer for something that could be cooked straight away. I took out some fishcakes and put them in the Aga then made a salad. After pouring myself another glass of wine, I went back into the sitting room. Peter would be starting work again tomorrow. He knew what needed to be done so I would just leave him to it. I pictured his face and strong hands and thought about the moment he touched my arm. Seconds later, a tingling sensation spread over my scalp. For a moment I thought he was in the room. I opened my eyes half expecting to see him, but I was alone. The experience was brief but it startled me. Perhaps I'd drunk too much wine. I took the empty glass into the kitchen and put it in the dishwasher then served up my meagre meal. As I ate, I thought about my website. The inspiration for my relishes had come from both Ali and Peter, although it was Peter who'd given me the idea for using Culpeper's ingenious ingredients. For some reason he kept occupying my thoughts. I had always considered myself to be intuitive in that I sometimes knew when the phone was about to ring, or when someone I hadn't heard from for a while would email me. I sensed he was thinking about me and I wondered in what way. There had never been any physical attraction between us, so it was unlikely to be that. Maybe he just felt concerned about me.

It had been a long day and I was too tired to think clearly about work, so I loaded everything into the dishwasher and turned it on, leaving it to swish behind me as I switched off the light and closed the door.

My alarm clock failed to go off and I woke to the sound of a truck engine idling outside before it fell silent. It was Peter. I looked at the time. It was eight-thirty. Clare would arrive at ten so I had plenty of time to prepare for the day. I lay on my back and listened to the gate opening and closing then to the heavy footsteps walking along the path behind the house until they became more distant as they

176

climbed the steps to the shed. He would have noticed the curtains still being closed so would probably try not to disturb me. I stretched then reluctantly got out of my warm bed to take a shower. The weather had turned colder and when I opened the curtains, saw a heavy, grey sky. I pulled a thick, roll-neck sweater out of the drawer and tugged it over my head. The barn never really got warm despite the additional heat from the stoves.

I went downstairs and was just passing the study when the phone rang. It was Beth.

'Hello Susie. I thought I'd call rather than text. I get irritated with all this messaging. It's nice to have human contact too sometimes. I'm pleased you can come for lunch on Saturday.' At first her voice was warm and friendly but then she sounded concerned as though she knew Adam and I had gone our separate ways. 'I've been thinking about you a lot lately. I'm so sorry not to have seen you over Christmas. Are you okay?'

'Yes, I'm fine thanks,' I said trying to sound upbeat. 'What time shall I come over?'

'Shall we say 12pm? Steve won't be here so it'll be just the two of us.'

'I'll look forward to it. We can catch up then. I must go as I need to get on with a few things.' I heard her quickly say something else, but I didn't answer and ended the call.

Before leaving the house, I lit the wood burner and left the kitchen door open so that the Aga and the fire would keep everything warm until I returned. I wanted to devote the rest of the day to writing about my business. Maybe I'd get a quote or two from Peter and perhaps a photo of him, if he'd let me.

I put on my quilted jacket, a pair of gloves and my blue woolly hat then ventured out into the cold. The wind was biting and my nose instantly froze. Peter was laying a section of hedge behind the barn. He'd lit a bonfire to burn the wood he'd cut away and also to keep warm. Ash and smoke drifted skyward at first and then sideways with the wind – the sweet, charred smell reminding me of everything I liked about winter. I walked over to where he was working.

'Good job you've got that fire going. It's freezing today, isn't it?' I said. He turned round with a start as if he'd been preoccupied.

'Hello Susie. Yes, but I think all this physical activity will keep me warm too.' He continued to hack at the hedge with his bill-hook. 'How are you today?'

I realised he was referring to the episode in the barn. 'Busy....new orders to fulfil and a new website to set up, with some help from one of my customers.'

'It seems as though your business is going from strength to strength. I'm pleased for you.' He stopped working and stood facing me. I tried to avoid eye contact with him.

'Have you thought about what you might do if things really took off?'

'Find a manufacturer that could produce my relish on a much larger scale, I suppose, but I'm hoping that won't happen. I'd like the business to grow but in a manageable way. It's a cottage industry and that's how I want it to stay.' I then remembered I was going to write something about him. 'By the way, would you mind if I mentioned you on the website and how you inspired me?'

'Yes I would, actually – please don't,' he said, turning away from me as if I'd offended him.

'Why?'

'Because I don't want you to, that's all.'

'I won't mention you by name. I'll just say my gardener ....'

'No Susie. I said no, and I mean no. There's no need to say anything about me. Ideas can come from anywhere. You'll have to think of something else.' His reaction surprised me. It made me wonder if he had something to hide.

'Okay. Sorry, I thought you wouldn't mind. You're right, there's no need to mention you. I'll make something up.' I walked away towards the barn feeling disappointed

178

and bewildered. As I unlocked the door, I looked back at him but he was barely visible through the haze of smoke. I just couldn't work him out at all.

Giles was due to turn up at ten o'clock. Clare had agreed to pose for a few shots, looking just the part in her red apron and white catering cap. I'd managed to capture her chopping vegetables, stirring one of the pots on the stove and filling a jar with relish. They all looked great, but I wondered if I'd taken enough.

His knock at the front door was barely audible above the radio which I quickly turned off. I let him into the sitting room.

'Great to see you again Susie,' he said kissing me on the right cheek. It was unexpected and I blushed.

'And you. How are things?'

'..Okay – there seems to be a post-festive lull at the moment but that's to be expected. Everyone goes on a diet in January – which is why I've got some free time.'

He took off his jacket and I hung it up for him.

'What a great place,' he said, glancing up at the beamed ceiling and then around the room. 'How long have you lived here?'

'Twelve years.' I really didn't want to talk about the house and hoped he wouldn't ask too many questions. It was still too painful. 'I've made some fresh coffee, would you like some?'

'That would be nice, thanks,' he said, lowering himself into the armchair near the wood burner. He leaned forward and held out the palms of his hands towards the fire. There was something very endearing and childlike about him, which made me feel motherly, even though I'd never experienced motherhood. I went into the kitchen.

As I poured the coffee, he came through the door.

'I hope you don't mind. I just wanted to have a look round. This is really homely,' he said casting his eyes over my colourful collection of pottery. 'I can sense you've been really happy here.'

179

'Yes, I have but things have changed,' I said, trying to hint at my newfound circumstances and that life wasn't a bed of roses any more.

'I'm sorry. I shouldn't have been so tactless – you living alone, and all that.'

I'd never mentioned being widowed so let him assume whatever he wanted to.

'I think we'd better get down to business,' I said. 'I'll show you what I've done so far.' He followed me into the study and I opened the articles I'd written and showed him the photos. He sat down in front of the computer and scrolled through the pages. I watched his eyes moving swiftly from side to side across the screen.

'This looks good. There are some sites that let you create a website for free. I think they might be your best option if you don't want anything too complicated. It's just a case of deciding on the links then adding the relevant information,' he said confidently.

'I'm afraid computers still baffle me,' I replied sounding like a complete technophobe.

'Okay, leave it to me. I'll see what I can come up with.'
'Thanks. That would be great.' I was relieved to be let off the hook so easily. 'I need to go and check on Clare. I'll be back in a few minutes.'

I removed his empty coffee cup from the desk and took it back to the kitchen then made my way up to the barn. A thin wisp of smoke curled up from Peter's bonfire which had now been reduced to a pile of smouldering embers. I looked over to where he'd been working but there was no sign of him so I went down to the paddock where he normally took a break but he wasn't there either. Then I noticed that his tools had gone so I went to the part of the garden where I could see over to the parking bay next to the house. It was empty. I glanced at my watch. It was only eleven o'clock. He wasn't due to go until twelve. A pang of guilt rose up inside me. He rarely left without saying goodbye. I thought of calling him but decided to wait. Maybe he'd gone to get something and would come

180

back. It worried me to think I might have upset him.

When I walked into the barn, Clare was putting on her coat. I'd forgotten she had a dental appointment. She'd made up a batch of relishes that needed to cool before being put into boxes.

'You're a star,' I said. 'We ought to go out for dinner one evening. It will be my treat – to thank you for all your hard work.'

'That would be wonderful Susie. I expect Alfie could survive one evening without me. He does fret when I go out though,' she said.

I recalled the time I visited her and how he'd howled when she shut him in another room. Dogs demand so much attention and I was glad not to own one, despite friends saying they're great company. There was a lot to be said for freedom too.

'Let's think of where to go and talk about it tomorrow,' I said as she was leaving.

'Good idea. See you in the morning.'

I followed her out and closed the door then went back to the house. Giles was still busy so I went into the kitchen. Peter's disappearance disturbed me. I couldn't understand why he should get so upset about being on a website. Practically everyone uses social media these days. I'd never been that interested in his background before, but now I wanted to know everything about him – where he came from; who he knew; where he'd worked; how old he was; if he had any relatives. All I knew for sure was that he looked after his father and believed in God. He'd never volunteered information about himself, but I respected that. Suddenly the idea of delving into his private life seemed wrong. Perhaps I should leave well alone. He'd only ever shown me kindness and I needed his support. I picked up my phone and dialled his number which immediately clicked into his answering service. I hadn't thought about what to say so I ended the call.

At that moment Giles peered round the door. 'If you've got a moment Susie, I'd like to show you what I've done.'

'Yes, of course.' I followed him back to the study.

Chapter 18

I'd left three messages on Peter's answerphone over three consecutive days and still not heard from him, but I was sure he would eventually call. He just wasn't the sort of man to let me down. I wasn't expecting him to work again until the following Tuesday, so thought it best to wait and see if he turned up. I tried to put him out of my mind but every so often he would re-emerge and I'd go over the same old pattern of reasoning. There had to be a rational explanation for his lack of contact. Perhaps he'd gone home because he felt ill. It was odd, but in all the time we'd known each other, he'd never told me where he lived, and I'd never bothered to ask. He once mentioned he was staying a few miles down the road so that narrowed it down to two villages, one of which was Hatch End. If all else failed, I could ask Mike, the landlord of the Three Horseshoes if he knew him.

The walk to Beth's cottage took longer than usual. Patches of ice had formed on the lane. There was no wind and the only sound came from my footsteps. I looked up at the trees, but there was no sign of life. It was too cold.

Beth's drive was steeper than I remembered and by the time I reached the top, I was out of breath. I stopped for a while to recover before walking towards the front door. A wave of nostalgia drifted over me as I relived her anniversary party and the moment Adam and I had first caught sight of each other in the marquee. Since Christmas I'd tried to bury all thoughts of him and focus on my business but returning to where we'd met brought everything back and I wondered if I could cope with being questioned about him. The thought of having lunch with Beth now seemed like a bad idea and I wanted to go home, but it was too late. She must have seen me through the window and opened the door.

'... Susie. Come in, come in. It's lovely to see you

183

again.'

We went into her cosy sitting room where the warmth of a large open fire filled the room. She then asked how I was and for a moment I couldn't answer, but then I said, 'fine thanks' and sat down.

She started to talk about her family Christmas and how wonderful it had been to have everyone together again. I'd never been part of a large, close-knit family so it was hard to imagine – and then I remembered the happiness that you and I had shared at Christmas, but now it all seemed so distant and unreal. Recent events had left me feeling drained.

Instead of listening to what she had to say, I found myself concentrating on the musical lilt of her soft west-country accent. She must have noticed my distraction.

'I'm sorry – I got carried away. Let me get you something Susie – a nice gin and tonic perhaps?'

'Actually, that would be great, thank you.'

Apart from the crackling of burning logs, and the ticking from an old wall clock, the room was quiet and I leant back in my armchair. The furniture had seen better days and a thin layer of dust covered the table tops. Despite its shabbiness, the room felt well-loved and homely. Family photos and memorabilia filled the shelves in the alcoves beside the inglenook and a number of original paintings of animals and landscapes hung on the uneven walls. One in particular stood out and I got up to look at it more closely. It was of a black Labrador lying on a red carpet. The artist's name, Ben Fuller, didn't mean anything to me but the way he'd captured the expression in its eyes and the sheen of its coat were remarkably life-like. Beth came back with a small tray of drinks and held it towards me. The ice chinked against the side of the glass as I picked it up. 'I love your painting of the Labrador. What a beautiful dog.'

'Yes, that was Barney. He was fourteen when he died. We keep thinking about getting another dog. I suppose we will eventually.'

I wanted to continue talking about anything other than myself, no matter how trivial, but Beth looked impatient and I could see she was keen to know how I'd coped with Christmas. 'Before you ask Beth, I'm not with Adam anymore and our Christmas was a disaster, so now we've got that out of the way, I hope we can talk about more important things.'

'Oh.' Her face fell and for the first time since I'd known her, she was speechless. 'Actually, I did know about you and Adam, and I'm sorry things didn't work out, but it wasn't your fault. It was Jane's. She wouldn't leave him alone until she got him back.'

'Beth, please. Whatever has happened, it's in the past. Let it go. I don't want to talk about it. Adam and I weren't meant to be and that's that.' In the silence that followed, I thought about the phone call on Boxing Day when we were walking down to the beach. It had obviously been Jane not his daughter, and then it occurred to me that they had probably met, even slept together. The idea that she had shared his bed made me feel sick. I took a large swig of my drink and felt the liquid slide down my throat like a dose of cold medicine.

'I suppose I'm kidding myself that things are getting better. My business is doing well and I hang onto that. It's the only positive thing in my life at the moment.'

Beth reached over and put her hand on top of mine. 'You've done so remarkably well considering all you've been through, my dear. I really don't know how you've managed.'

'I don't know either Beth, but somehow you find the strength to carry on.' At that moment, an image of Peter entered my mind and, for some unknown reason, it made me smile.

'Well, that's the spirit. Let's go and have some lunch.' We went into the kitchen and I sat at the large, pine table while Beth cut up one of her delicious, home-made cheese and bacon quiches. She put a long, thin baguette on a bread board and handed me a knife. I cut off a few pieces and put them in a bread basket. The smell reminded me of the freshly-baked bread my mother used to make and made my mouth water. Being with Beth in her kitchen always seemed to bring back childhood memories. It had the comforting warmth of happy family life with something appetising constantly baking in the oven. It reminded me so much of the one I grew up in. Even looking at her now from behind, I could visualise my mother doing the very same things. The thought hung in my mind until the emptiness of my life hit home. I kept myself busy to avoid thinking about it, but now, as I sat near someone who exuded contentment, it was painfully apparent how lonely my life had become. Without having someone to love, it seemed meaningless.

Beth brought the quiche and a bowl of salad to the table and put it next to the bread.

'Do help yourself Susie. Can I get you something else to drink?' She picked up my empty glass.

'Just some water would be fine, thanks,' I replied.

She returned with a bottle of wine as well as some water. 'Are you sure I can't tempt you with a glass? It's a very good sauvignon blanc.'

'Okay then, just one – thanks.' I'd not really drunk very much since Adam and I had gone our separate ways – just the occasional glass of wine at the end of a busy day, but I liked Beth's company and it would be impolite to let her drink alone.

'So what are you planning to do for your next fundraising event?' I asked, thinking back to the previous summer fair.

'It's going to be a concert in the garden. I'm asking people to bring their own food and drink, plus a chair or rug to sit on and wondered if you could sell raffle tickets this time, as well as your relishes? I won't be asking Adam and Jane, but if they get to hear about it and want to buy tickets, I'm afraid I won't be able to say no.'

'Don't worry – I'm quite capable of defending myself,' I replied, dreading the thought. They were bound to come.

It would be a way of showing people they were back together. Damn them. Beth was staring at me as if she was trying to work out what I was thinking. I looked down at my plate and pushed my food around before plunging my fork into a small, ripe tomato. 'Who's playing?' I asked, hoping for something lively and loud that people could dance to.

'I thought I'd go for a bit of soul – something a bit funky. Have you heard of The Flying Pigs Blues Band?'

I shook my head but smiled to show my approval. 'They sound perfect Beth – anything to liven up this quiet little backwater.' I thought of Giles and his wide circle of friends. 'Maybe I could ask some of my customers to advertise the event for you?'

'That's a wonderful idea. It won't be until June so we've got plenty of time to organise things.' Beth topped up my glass of wine without asking and I didn't stop her. 'Cheers Susie – to a prosperous New Year.'

'Absolutely,' I said, raising my glass and noticing she'd left out the word 'happy.'

After clearing away lunch, we went back to the sitting room and chatted for a while. It was five o'clock when Beth tapped me on the shoulder.

'Oh, I'm so sorry – how rude of me.' I opened my eyes and sat bolt upright. I'd fallen asleep.

'Don't you worry, my dear,' she said in her gentle, motherly voice. She'd turned on the table lamp next to me. It was dark outside.

'I'd better go. Thanks for a lovely lunch.' I ran my fingers through my hair then stood up and straightened my clothes before picking up my handbag. Beth helped me on with my jacket.

It was just about light enough to find my way home without a torch. The temperature had dropped and I tried to walk briskly, avoiding the patches of ice. I'd left the lights on in the cottage, assuming it might be late by the time I got back and, as it came into view, I was heartened to see the windows glowing against the night sky.

187

I'd been waiting since eight o'clock to hear the familiar sound of Peter's truck but he hadn't come. It annoyed me to think he could be so inconsiderate. Just a text to tell me what was going on would have put my mind at rest. He must have seen the missed calls from me. I dialled his number and, again, no answer. This time I sent a text. He was bound to reply to that.

I checked my emails. There was one from an address I didn't recognise but the subject – *'your products are of interest'* – caught my attention. I opened it and read quickly. *'I came across your website the other day and would like to sample some of your asparagus and white wine relish. I work as a buyer for Spears and Co. Please could you call me to discuss further...'* I was stunned. Spears and Co was one of the largest and most prestigious stores in the area. People travelled miles to shop there. It had started as a farm shop then grown into an organic supermarket selling locally grown food and its superb restaurant was always fully booked. I stood for a while contemplating what to do, then ran up to the barn to tell Clare who was quietly boxing up some orders.

'You won't believe this, but I've just been contacted by Spears and Co. They want to try my asparagus relish.'

At first she just stared at me, as if she hadn't understood and then she said,'Wow, that's fantastic. What on earth will we do if they place a big order?'

'Let's take things one step at a time. I'll have to approach a manufacturer capable of producing my relish on a much larger scale. We can do it on a contract basis. They make it for us and we sell it to customers. Don't worry, I've looked into it. I hadn't really wanted this to happen but now it has – business could really take off – we'll see.'

At that moment, the sound of a car slowly approaching along the gravel drive, made me go to the window. It was Steve. He'd come to do some deliveries.

'I must go and call the person from Spears. You can tell Steve my news on the basis that he keeps it to himself and doesn't even tell Beth.'

She answered in her usual pragmatic way, 'I think I'll wait until you've got that big order.'

'You're right. Let's go out tonight anyway and celebrate the possibility. I'll come and pick you up at seven and we can go down the road to my local.' The Three Horseshoes was as good a place as any and the food was always freshly-cooked.

'That should give me time to see to Alfie – sounds perfect.'

Steve walked in as I was about to leave. We chatted briefly and I pointed to the boxes that were stacked by the store cupboard, most of which were for Greens, and said that Clare had the paperwork. He looked surprised to see me in such high spirits and asked if I'd had some good news.

'Actually, yes,' I replied.

As I walked down the steps to the house, my thoughts returned to Peter. There was still no sign of him. I went into the study and checked my phone but there were no messages. It irritated me, but then I thought about his circumstances. Perhaps his father had been taken seriously ill, even died, and he hadn't had a chance to contact me. Of all the reasons, this seemed the most likely and I felt guilty for thinking badly of him. At least I would have a chance to do some investigating later at the pub. The bar staff were bound to have come across him at some stage.

The email from Spears and Co sat on my computer screen as I dialled the number for the preserves buyer, Carolyn Davis. She answered stating her name. I waited for her to say something else, but she didn't.

'Hello. I'm Susie Chester. You sent me an email expressing an interest in my asparagus and white wine relish. I....'

'Yes,' she interrupted, 'thanks for calling me back. Your product looks really interesting and I like the idea behind it. You say it's supposed to be an aphrodisiac.'

'Yes, at least that's what the herbalist Nicholas

Culpeper believed. Obviously the recipe had to be modified, but the main ingredients are white wine, white wine vinegar, orange zest, onions, spices and asparagus.'

'Could you send me a jar?' she asked. 'I'd love to try it.'

'Of course – I'll send you a couple today,' I said, realising that I could just as easily deliver them, but I had some ordering to do. She gave me her address and said she would get back to me as soon as she could.

I went back up to tell Clare and put a couple of jars in one of the gift boxes. My heart was pounding with excitement as well as apprehension, but I knew I would cope – it was just a case of finding the right manufacturer who could make my hand-made relish taste the same.

Apart from the regulars at the bar who go for a drink after work, the Three Horseshoes was almost empty. Our entrance caused a few heads to turn. Clare went to sit at a table by the window while I went to the bar. The row of men sitting with their backs to me looked like labourers and farm workers – their clothes splattered with mud or building dust. I looked along the line hoping that one of them might be Peter, but none of them had grey curly hair.

Mike, the landlord, smiled. 'What can I get you?'

I ordered Clare a pint of her favourite ale and something less alcoholic for me. He picked up a glass and tilted it under the tap then slowly pulled down the pump handle.

'I don't suppose you've ever come across a gardener called Peter, have you? I'm sorry but I don't know his surname. He lives locally.' It sounded a ridiculous question.

'Come to think of it, yes, I do. Is he tall, dark and slim, probably in his forties?'

'He's about three inches taller than me with grey curly hair. It doesn't matter. I just thought I'd ask.' At least he hadn't come back with some sarcastic remark.

One of the men at the bar looked at me and for a moment I thought he was going to say something, but then he looked away.

Clare was checking her phone. I put her beer on the table and sat down opposite her. It was as if I was invisible. She reached over for her drink without looking up.

'Well, any news from Tom?' I asked wanting her to realise she had company.

'Yes, but nothing important. He's coming home early on Friday.' She put her phone back in her bag and picked up the menu. 'This all looks good,' she said. 'I'm impressed. We've never eaten here before. Tom thinks it's too spit and sawdust, if you know what I mean.'

I couldn't answer. It was a country pub that was used by country people. Clare's elegant and meticulous dress sense made her stand out – from her designer black leather boots to her Cashmere sweater and neatly-cropped, auburn hair. She could have been a model and I wondered if Adam had told the truth about her. It seemed unlikely. With Tom away during the week, there was ample opportunity for her to play around. I tried to put the thought out of my mind. There was no point. I'd grown to like her and she was good at her job.

The evening passed amiably and the tables around us had gradually filled. Mike was struggling to cope, despite having two other bar staff to help him. The seats at the bar had been taken over by couples, but there was one man on his own at the far end sitting by the wall. His shoulders were hunched forward and his head was lowered as if he was focusing on his drink but from behind I could make out his wavy, grey hair.

'I'm just going to the loo, back in a minute.' I got up from the table and went to the cloakroom, pushing my way past a few people waiting to be served at the bar. The man in the corner had one hand clasped around his beer glass and the other resting on his knee. From his profile, I could see it wasn't Peter. His skin wasn't as weathered and his nose was too long and straight. He looked as though he wanted to be left alone. I stood next to him, trying to catch

191

Mike's attention so I could settle the bill. The man slowly turned his head towards me. His eyes were half closed and he tried to say something but the words were slurred. I decided to pay on my way back.

Clare thanked me for a lovely evening then got out of the car. She waved as I drove off and in my rear view mirror, I watched her go indoors. She'd had a lot to drink and I wondered how she'd feel in the morning. We'd had a good evening and I was glad we'd gone out together. I sensed she'd appreciated it too.

I arrived home ten minutes later. For some reason, the security lights didn't come on. I got out of the car and waited for my eyes to adjust to the darkness. It took several attempts to find the keyhole in the front door but eventually I managed to get into the house and turn on the sitting room lights. Relieved to be able to see again, I locked the door and closed the curtains. Even as an adult, I still had a fear of the dark – perhaps more so now I was alone. I went to the kitchen to get a glass of water then went upstairs to bed. The problem with the outside light could wait until tomorrow.

Having eaten a good meal, I expected to go straight to sleep but thoughts of Peter and the man at the bar kept me awake. There were similarities between them and I wondered if I should have spoken to him. He could have been a relative. Peter's whereabouts was plaguing me more than I realised, but I couldn't afford to lose sleep over it. If I didn't hear from him within the next couple of weeks, I'd look for another gardener. My patience was wearing thin.

In my heart of hearts, I knew Carolyn Davis would like my relish. Why shouldn't she? Everyone else did, so when I received her email asking me to come and see her, it didn't really surprise me. I'd managed to find a manufacturer that was willing to mass produce my relish and now felt excited at the prospect of seeing my business grow. My only concern was getting the ingredients right so that the taste wasn't altered in any way. I'd been told this would be a fairly lengthy process so I hoped that any order she placed would be to a manageable timescale. If all went according to plan, it was inevitable that my relish would end up being factory made. The thought of having to tell Clare and Steve they were no longer needed saddened me, but nothing was definite and, for now, their jobs were safe. I replied to Carolyn's email agreeing to meet her at ten o'clock the following Wednesday. Neither Clare nor Steve would be working that day so I was free to spend as much time with her as necessary. As I typed the last sentence, I remembered what Peter had said some months ago, 'you're a good person, Susie and good things are going to happen to you.' Despite the unbearable sadness of losing you and my misfortune with Adam, life *was* looking up. I felt positive, even happy. It had been a difficult journey but I now knew I was on the right road and, although friends had helped, in the end, it was Peter who had inspired me. I wanted to tell him about Spears and Co and that I was beginning to feel like my old self again, but most of all, I wanted to thank him.

I gazed through the window at the garden. Even in the depths of winter, there was still structure and colour from the evergreen shrubs, the white trunks of the silver birch trees and red dogwood stems. The lawn also looked fresh and green. Peter had always worked quietly and methodically – a gentle, hardworking man who had always put my feelings first – which was why his disappearance just didn't make sense. Although there were more important things to think about, I knew I had to try and find him somehow.

Chapter 19

I had often visited Spears and Co. just to browse. Sometimes I'd be tempted to buy something but the high-quality range of food was expensive and not somewhere I could afford to shop on a regular basis. Unlike other supermarkets, there were no aisles to walk down which made it look less stark and clinical, and all the products were within easy reach.

I still had ten minutes to spare before my meeting, so I walked around to get a feel of the place. It reminded me of a chic country market. Everything looked colourful and tempting, including the butcher's counter with its white tiled surfaces and stainless steel trays full of fresh, organic meats. Customers were queuing to be served by three men dressed in blue and white striped aprons. One was cooking sausages in a cast iron frying pan then cutting them up for people to try. I picked up one of the pieces with a cocktail stick and put it in my mouth. The main flavours were pork and spices, but there was also a hint of fruit, which was confirmed by the label in front of the plate saying 'pork and red onion marmalade.' I complimented him and vowed to come back later to buy some.

The relish section comprised of six large stands. Most were produced locally or from the surrounding counties and I wondered how mine would fare against such strong competition. I hadn't expected such a huge variety.

Carolyn's office was along a corridor at the back of the store. I looked at the names on each of the doors as I walked past. Hers was at the far end. I composed myself then knocked a couple of times and a soft but assertive voice called me in.

'You must be Susie, hi, nice to meet you,' she said standing up and moving towards me, holding out her right hand. She was the same height as me but plump with brown, shoulder-length hair and hazel eyes framed by a pair of black-rimmed glasses. I reciprocated and shook her hand then looked at the large table where three other young people were sitting. She introduced me to them in turn. The head of sales and marketing was a thirty-something year-old man called Brian with probing green eyes who, I sensed, had summed me up before I'd even sat down. A jar of my relish sat diminutively in the centre.

Carolyn started the meeting by praising its concept. Heads nodded in agreement and then its properties were discussed which prompted some nervous laughter, but it was generally accepted that it was bound to have wide appeal. I told the group how much the demand for my relish had grown in just eight months and the turnover I'd achieved. Again, more nods of approval, then Brian asked why I hadn't expanded the range and I explained how I had but the other flavours hadn't really taken off. He quickly dismissed this and said that anything which suggested health benefits had great potential. After almost an hour it was decided to trial my relish with an order for two hundred jars. I'd expected more but it was a start. At least I now had a foothold in the most prestigious store in the county.

Carolyn walked me back through the store until we reached the sliding, glass doors at the front. We shook hands again and she said she would confirm everything in writing.

Franco's was unusually busy. I stood in the queue and looked around for somewhere to sit – and then, as I glanced towards the back of the café – I noticed a figure I immediately recognised sitting at a small table reading a newspaper. From his ruddy complexion and grey hair, I knew it was Peter. Contrary to everything I'd imagined, he looked relaxed and contented, as if he didn't have a care in the world. I watched him lift his coffee cup to his lips without taking his eyes off what he was reading. He seemed oblivious to everything around him. What was he playing at? My surprise turned to anger which churned away inside me until I couldn't contain it. I slipped out of the queue and walked over to his table.

'Long time no see,' I said abruptly.

He glanced up and smiled. 'Susie – it's good to see you. I've been meaning to call you…'

'..Oh – really. Why didn't you then?'

'It's been difficult. Look, why don't you get something to drink and come and join me. I'll explain everything.' His soft brown eyes begged forgiveness.

'Okay, I'll be back as soon as I can.' The queue had grown and was snaking its way almost to the entrance. It would take a while to be served, but at least I had somewhere to sit.

The extensive, hand-written menu was displayed on a large blackboard which hung on the wall behind the counter. I chose a lasagne and green salad then waited, and waited until eventually a harassed barista asked for my order. He put my coffee and a glass of water on a small tray then gave me a number for the food. I picked up some cutlery and a napkin then manoeuvred my way back to Peter's table.

As I was approaching, I stopped. He'd gone – and someone else had taken his place. I stood holding my tray, too shocked to say anything, but the man gestured for me to sit down.

'It looks like that's the last empty seat so please take it.'

'If you're sure you don't mind,' I said, still dazed by Peter's disappearance. It was like some sort of magic trick. 'I don't suppose you saw the man sitting where you are leave, did you? He was here just a few minutes ago.' I noticed that Peter's paper had been folded up and put to one side.

'No, sorry,' he replied, looking at me as though he'd not really understood what I'd said. There was something familiar about him. I sat down and emptied the contents of my tray on to the table then put it on the floor against the wall. I sipped my coffee and tried to work out what had just happened. For a moment, I thought I'd imagined talking to Peter but his paper was proof that I hadn't. Maybe he'd changed his mind and didn't want to tell me about his recent difficulties or perhaps he was embarrassed about not contacting me? I was confused and bewildered, but having ordered some food, I couldn't just get up and go. The man was reading a phone message; a few strands of his dark hair fell forward as he looked down. I tried to recall where I might have seen him before, and then I remembered. It was in Green's, just before Christmas. He was standing by my relish display and had obviously read the magazine article because he'd joked about wanting my autograph. At the time, I'd not given it much thought but later, when I was driving home, I realised I should have got to know him better. He was attractive and amusing.

Now sitting in such close proximity to him, I felt I ought to start a conversation but, apart from saying something banal like 'haven't we met somewhere before?' I couldn't think of anything, so I glanced over towards the kitchen to see if my food was on its way. While my head was turned, I sensed he was studying me and when I turned back he was still looking at me. I tried to avoid eye contact so focused on my coffee.

'I'm still waiting too,' he said loudly, trying to make himself heard above the constant chatter.

'Yes, I was beginning to think I shouldn't have come here. It's always like this at lunch times.'

'Well, thankfully, I'm not in a hurry,' he said.

We continued our conversation in a light-hearted way. There was an instant rapport between us which reminded me of when you and I had first met.

The Italian waitress apologised for the delay as she put our food on the table. Her bubbly personality made it difficult not to forgive her and, as she walked away, we started to talk about our shared love of everything Italian, from its architecture and culture to its unfathomable politics. After we'd finished eating, he sat back in his chair. 'I've been thinking where I've seen you before and it's just come to me. You were in Green's around

Christmas, weren't you? I'd just read the article about your relish and then you came along. I'm delighted to meet you again. Susie, isn't it? I'm Richard Lewis,' he said holding out his hand over the table which I quickly shook. We'd been talking for almost an hour and only just got round to introducing ourselves. 'Susie Chester. Good to meet you too.' This time I looked into his blue-grey eyes. They seemed to draw me in.

'So how's business?' he asked.

'At the moment, it's going very well – and how about you? What's your line of work?'

'I'm a retired dentist.' He smiled as if to illustrate his recent profession.

Our conversation flowed easily from one topic to another until the café had become almost empty. We looked around conscious that we ought to go but hesitated and then he said, 'Are you married?'

'Widowed,' I replied. '….Just over a year ago.'

'I'm divorced – been on my own for four years.'

We looked at each other in anticipation and then he said, 'Would you like to meet up again?'

'Yes, I would,' I replied.

Meeting Richard Lewis was one of those rare moments of being in the right place at the right time. In just one day, all the crumbled ruins of the past had suddenly been reassembled. My life had been turned around. I could feel the sun again and its warmth surging through me. I wanted to laugh and shout and tell the world that everything was okay. It really was. There was only one piece of the puzzle still missing and that was Peter.

Richard and I spent as much time as we could together. It was always hard to part, but the demands of my business had escalated and it was better for me to work long into the night on my own. Orders kept increasing and the time had come to switch to mass production. It had taken several weeks to perfect the taste of my relish but, in the end, I had succeeded and the end result was almost preferable to the original.

A part of the barn had been turned into an office where Clare and I now worked and the stoves lay unused. Steve helped in the garden as much as he could. It seemed unlikely that Peter was ever coming back, but on the days he was due to work, I still listened out for his truck.

It was the beginning of March but despite the white carpet of snowdrops, and the early shoots of daffodils, it was still exceptionally cold. A northerly wind and the threat of snow made me want to stay at home. A mass of dark grey clouds had gathered out to the west indicating a storm was imminent. I peered through the window from the warmth of my kitchen and decided not to venture further than the barn. Steve had come early to pick up some urgent orders. I just hoped he'd get back home before the weather changed.

It was midday when the first flakes of snow began to fall. They drifted slowly and silently past the kitchen window until they landed gently on the frozen ground. Richard had left at eight o'clock and wouldn't be coming back until Thursday. I wondered now if that would be possible. I called Clare and told her not to come to work tomorrow. We could do everything by email. I then called Richard who had made it home safely. We were missing each other already.

It had been a long time since I'd spent the day alone but I had work to do. I sat down in an armchair to collect my thoughts and, every now and then, glanced through the window. The white flakes were falling with more intensity and I knew that by tomorrow, there would be deep snow outside. The cottage was six hundred feet above sea level so the weather was always more severe, but the roads were usually kept passable by local farmers who still needed to work.

It was hard to imagine life in nearby towns and cities carrying on as normal, but despite being isolated, I no longer felt lonely. Too much had changed. I had changed. There was still sadness from time to time, but it was far less painful.

As I walked across the room towards the study, I glanced upwards. There seemed so much to live for now, I couldn't help saying 'thank you.' I wasn't sure who or what I was thanking, but it didn't matter. I just needed to say it.

The afternoon passed quickly with numerous phone calls and a long list of emails to answer. One of them was from Sophie Williams who wanted to know if she could write another article about my business. She was now working for an upmarket food magazine. I responded by saying I'd put something together and send it to her and if she needed any more information, to call me. Publicity hadn't been a priority but I welcomed the chance to raise my profile at Spears and Co.

When I finally turned off my computer, it was seven o'clock. The house was unusually silent. I went into the sitting room to close the curtains and was immediately struck by the amount of snow that had settled against the window. I put my face against the pane of glass until I could see the deep, white blanket that now lay outside

The fire in the wood burner had almost died so I opened the vent and put some kindling on the embers until it came back to life. I sat on the rug to watch the flames take hold then put on a few logs. It was so comforting I stayed for a while absorbing the heat until I almost fell asleep. It was only my hunger that made me eventually get up and go into the kitchen to find something to eat.

The next morning, I woke to bright sunshine. I got up and wrapped myself in my dressing gown before going downstairs. Richard had sent a text asking me to call him. He wanted to know if I was okay and if I had enough food. He had obviously decided that, as I was now cut off from the rest of the world, I might starve. I called him, but there was no answer so I sent a text to assure him that I wouldn't go hungry – not with neighbours like Beth and Steve just down the road.

The sun flooded the sitting room as I opened the

curtains and the brilliant white landscape almost took my breath away. It looked so crisp and clean against the clear blue sky. I ran upstairs, took a quick shower then put on the warmest clothes I could find.

As I pulled on my wellingtons, a large clump of snow slid off the roof and landed outside the back door. I wondered how deep it would be and if my boots were long enough. I put on my jacket and a pair of gloves then braced myself, and opened the door. The icy air hit the back of my throat. The snow wasn't as deep as I thought but deep enough to leave a neat trail of footprints in my wake. I walked round to the patio, or to where it should have been. A thick, powdery layer of snow covered the tables and chairs and the top of the well. I stood still. There was no sound. It was beautiful.

I was staring down the valley when I heard the gate open and close. Someone was walking towards me. The sun was so bright I had to shield my eyes to see who it was.

'Hello Susie.'

'Peter. What are you doing here?'

'I had to come and see you.....'

I was stunned that he was standing there in front of me after all this time. So much so, I couldn't speak.

'I'm so sorry. Things have been very difficult, but I had to come and tell you that I'm going away.'

'I gathered you weren't coming back, but I'd have appreciated a phone call. I've been so worried about you.'

'But you don't understand. I couldn't tell you until now. There's nothing more for me to do here. I've done everything that I needed to. I have to go.'

He was right. I didn't understand, but too much time had gone by so I resisted persuading him to stay. 'I'm sorry you're leaving, but I expect I'll manage somehow.'

'Of course you will,' he said.

In all the time I had known him, I'd rarely seen him look sad, but at that moment he looked close to tears. I wanted to put my arms around him but I couldn't. 'I have a lot to thank you for, Peter and I'll miss you.'

He didn't say anything. He just stared at me and then he started to smile. It was a smile that radiated so much joy, it made me smile too.

'I get the feeling you've always known how things would turn out, haven't you?' I said.

'Yes Susie, I have.' His voice was soft and warm. 'I've known from the day I first met you.'

I absorbed each word now realising what they meant. For a while we just stood facing each other and then he picked up my hand and held it between his. It was the first truly affectionate gesture that had passed between us and I didn't know whether to laugh or cry.

'Thank you – thank you so much – for everything,' I said.

He gently let go of my hand. 'Goodbye, Susie.'

My heart sank as I watched him walk towards the gate which he opened and closed with his head bowed. He then stepped out onto the lane and made his way carefully up the hill without looking back. As he neared the top, he raised his right arm and waved – and then he was gone. At that moment, a large, dark cloud obscured the sun. I glanced up at the sky. A few flakes of snow began to fall. One looked larger than the others. I held out my hand and watched it land gently in the middle of my palm – it was a feather – a pure, white feather.

ACKNOWLEDGEMENTS

With grateful thanks to my creative writing tutors Lucy English, Patricia Wasrvedt and Tim Liardet, and my colleagues Kim Bour and Gill Eve for their invaluable help and guidance. Also to Julie Cornwell, Jayne Homer, Carolyn Hughes and Marie Doddy for their encouragement, and my sister Joyce and her husband Mike for their unfailing support. Lastly, my deepest thanks and love go to my Faroese mother who has always been there for me at the best and worst of times.

About the author

Sam Hayward

Sam grew up in Hampshire and after an administrative career, returned to full-time education to study Journalism. She graduated in 1997 with a BA (Hons) from Southampton Solent University and subsequently worked as a publications officer for a local cancer charity.

In 2000, she moved to Somerset with her husband, a retired Naval Commander, and worked as a part-time sub-editor for a regional newspaper.

In September 2013, she completed a postgraduate course in Creative Writing at Bath Spa University. Her debut novel *Black to White* was inspired by the loss of her husband to cancer in 2008.

For further information visit
www.sam-hayward.co.uk